SUCH IS M

The life of Antony Wood
Newcelles and tl.
2nd Earl Rivers.

His life was one of chivalry, power play - and death.

Dorothy Davies

SUCH IS MY DANCE

DEDICATION

Dedicated to the memory of

Antony Wydeville, K.G
Lord Scales of Newcelles and the Isle of Wight, 2nd Earl Rivers,
21st June 1442 - 25th June 1483
Executed without trial.
You will not be forgotten.
Requiescat in Pace.

And to the memory of
Jean Charles de Menezes
7th January 1978 - 22nd July 2005
Executed without trial.
You will not be forgotten.
Requiescat in Pace.

Antony wishes to dedicate this book to:

My much-loved family, starting with my parents, Richard and Jacquetta and moving on to all my many siblings. We were close when living and are close even now.

Dorothy's Mayan guide Redwood, for all the guidance freely given from the moment I walked into
Dorothy's life. He has been a virtual tower of strength to me.

Prince Ivan Grozny for guidance, friendship and so much more.

Dorothy's friend Mary who has put up with so much of my nonsense and will no doubt continue to go on doing it, God willing.

Dorothy's friend Terry for all his support, care and consideration for her, this one I love so much, and for accepting me.

Dorothy's companions, guides, helpers and those she thinks of as her team mates for their acceptance, laughter, understanding and love.

And most of all to Dorothy herself, for her love, her strength, her willingness to give me all that I need as a spirit and for all the work of writing my story. She spent countless hours researching my life before the decision was made to make this a channelled book rather than a formal biography and goodness knows how much money she spent in acquiring articles, prints and information. Her dedication to my cause and that of every spirit author who has approached her is way above and beyond the call of duty. She is my wife and I am proud to acknowledge her as such. We shared a life in the 15th century; we share a life now. I call her Rose for she is my rose, my precious love.

Earl Rivers.

Ballad written by Antony Wydeville, KG, Lord Scales of Newcelles and the Isle of Wight, 2nd Earl Rivers, on the 23rd June 1483 whilst in Sheriff-Hutton Castle, awaiting execution.

Somewhat musing
And more mourning,
In remembering
Th'unsteadfness;
This world being
Of such wheeling,
Me contrarying,
What may I guess?

I fear, doubtless,
Remediless,
Is now to seize
My woeful chance;
For unkindness,
Withoutenless,
And no redress,
Me doth advance.

With displeasure,
To my grievance,
And no surance
Of remedy;
Lo, in this trance,
Now in substance,
Such is my dance,
Willing to die.

Methinks truly
Bounden am I,
And that greatly,
To be content;
Seeing plainly

Fortune doth wry
All contrary
From mine intent.

My life was lent
Me to one intent.
It is nigh spent.
Welcome, Fortune!
But I ne went [never thought]
Thus to be shent [ruined]
But she it meant;
Such is her won. [custom]

'Tis all a Chequer-board of Nights and Days
Where Destiny with Men for Pieces plays:
Hither and thither moves, and mates, and slays,
And one by one back in the Closet lays.

Rubaiyat of Omar Khayyam

(Stanza chosen by Earl Rivers.)

It is noted that in the Preface to Malory's Morte de Arthur, William Caxton refers to 'one in specyal.' Scholars now believe that the 'one in specyal' is Antony Wydeville, KG, 2nd Earl Rivers, as it is believed this man of letters delivered the transcript of the book to Caxton with instructions to 'imprint the history of King Arthur.' He did not live to see the publication of the book.

On a late 16th or early 17th century manuscript can be found the words:

The Erle was the most
Lernyd valyant and
Honorable knight of
The world for his tyme
Yet all was exersid with
Adverse accydente in
His lyfe. At length cam
To atcheevge the honor
Of an undesarvid death.

From Immortality by John Drinkwater
Olton Pools, Sidgwick and Jackson Ltd., 1917

There in the midst of all these words shall be
Our names, our ghosts, our immortality.

Prologue

I was born on the 21st June 1442, had a wonderful childhood, an adventurous and dangerous life, two wonderful wives, lived in the most beautiful homes and held the highest offices in the land. On the 25th June 1483, four days after my 41st birthday, I walked out into the bright summer sunshine to lay my head on a block in order to have it severed from my body. I thought it then; I've said it since; that is one messy way to die. Blood everywhere; very undignified. They tell me it's an execution reserved for aristocrats. I say, bring on the peasantry, hanging would have been better, less gore.

That's a summary of my life. But, like most people, you'll want to know more than that; you'll want to know the whys and wherefores, the whole scenario of 15th century England. So that is what I'll give you.

England at that time was a divided nation; aristocracy and the rest of the population and never the two shall meet. Peasants, working people, went about their lives as they had always done, farming the land, scraping a living, being born, being buried, no matter who 'owned' the land they farmed or the houses in which they gave birth, lived their lives and died. Allegiance to their lord, the owner of the land, came as standard: they paid their rent to his rent collector and answered his call to arms when an array was issued because that was the way of life. If they died in battle for their lord, well, that too was part of life. You went to fight, you expected either to go home rich with looted items or to die, but at least you died a hero's death even if it was through being hacked to pieces by another Englishman. It seems incomprehensible to me now, at this distance of time, that major battles could be fought with hundreds if not thousands of men in armour or as armed as best they could be with bows, axes and spears, charging into the affray, hacking at their fellow men, bringing them down, suffocating them by fighting on and over their fallen bodies. All this whilst people in the surrounding countryside carried on their lives, not knowing – or caring – that such life and death confrontations were taking place.

Craftsmen pursued their many trades, blacksmiths, carpenters, mercers, cooks and many others, making a living in a time when a living was precarious for the political climate was ever changing and taxes could be imposed or increased at any moment, damaging livelihoods. Guilds were set up to protect the craftsmen as best they could, but even they were powerless before the sweeping changes brought in by a change of monarchy and a new set of laws.

The aristocracy, with their fine clothes, big houses and seemingly immense wealth were a world away from the average land-working people of England. The aristocracy fought each other, sometimes politely, sometimes savagely, for land, positions, money and possessions. Great homes, castles, estates, were sometimes the gift of the reigning monarch, sometimes deeded by family, sometimes acquired by marriage settlements. Catching the king's attention, being on the winning side in one of the many battles fought across the land or marrying well to gain property and titles was a way of life. Fashion was slavishly followed even if it appeared foolish, for example, the long pointed toes on men's shoes and the plucked hairlines to create very high foreheads for ladies seem strange even by medieval standards. Yet we went along with it, because it was wise to do so. The one thing you didn't do was stand out.

A strict hierarchy was in place among aristocrats: the king's permission had to be sought for a marriage and there were rigid rules about who took precedence over whom at banquets and State occasions. The person appointed to carry the train of a queen or to hold a child at a christening told the rest of the society how high you were in the king or queen's favour.

Once there, once breathing the heady atmosphere that was the intrigue of court, people were almost prisoners, having to seek the king's permission to be excused Court to attend to business, for example, or go on a pilgrimage. Life was controlled to a very great degree by the reigning monarch. Families relied on him for their income, for clothing, for shelter and support and in turn he dictated their lives in many respects.

Kings were expected to marry well, with the intention that the marriage should create or reinforce treaties with other countries, cement relationships between monarchs to avoid future problems and bring wealth and power to both sides. Dukes and Earls likewise were expected to marry into money or landed wealth to bring greater prosperity to the family.

Loyalty to one's lord and one's liege lord, the king, should have been taken for granted but unfortunately human beings are fickle creatures, led by many different emotions, everything from lust to jealousy. The best-laid plans of many an aristocrat were often overturned in a moment. Executions were considered normal and death was a constant, either through disease or fighting. Battles were a way of gaining glory, if you were on the winning side. Assignations were indiscreet and all but expected if you were a real 'man-about-Court'.

The ruling monarch at the time this story begins was the devout and mentally unstable Henry VI, a Lancastrian monarch, a man more fitted to the life of seclusion in the cloisters than the ravages of monarchy with all its many problems. These problems were enhanced by his powerful, ambitious, scheming wife, Margaret of Anjou, who held the monarchy together but whose machinations caused many difficulties. There were ambitious claimants to the throne of England; they too added their share to the difficulties besetting the royalty and aristocrats of England.

Taken overall, it was a time of courtly courtesy and conspiracy, power play and paranoia, chivalry and charlatans, knights and knaves, masques and manoeuvrings, dances and death.

Chapter 1 - Early life and family

I came into this uncertain, ever-changing world on the 21st June 1442: born to Richard Wydeville, Knight, and his wife Jacquetta of Luxemburg, dowager Duchess of Bedford, in a manor house in the sleepy village of Grafton in Northamptonshire. It didn't feel like a sleepy village to me for some years, but then, for some of it I was nothing more than a sleepy baby.

I think of tiny me, wrapped in swaddling bands and laid in my cradle in the corner of the room while the midwife and ladies attended to my mother. I didn't know I was destined for high rank and power in the medieval world, someone who would become a person demonstrating a startling array of talents (I say this with all modesty) and one who, ultimately, would clash with the person who could – and did – order my death. But that was in the future. Before then I could sleep without fore-knowledge of the great state occasions, the tournaments, the Court celebrations, the countries to be visited and the translating work to come. In many ways it was just as well I did not know that the 'storms of fortune' – to quote words from my book - would crash over me. Sometimes I feel it is best that people do not know what lies ahead of them, for surely they would not wish to walk the path of Life if they did.

This book is a chance for me to set the record straight on about a million mistakes which have crept into history books – all right, that might be a small exaggeration, we are not that well known a family – or are we? Let's make it 500,000 mistakes then, certainly it feels that way when I look at the books and sigh over yet another error, another mis-spelling of my name or another set of dates which don't match up with a) common sense and b) known facts.

We are Wydevilles. We are known as popinjays, traitors, usurpers and ambitious schemers. The name has come down through your history in a variety of ways and with a variety of descriptions attached to it:

Sympathetic: the hapless beautiful Elizabeth, Queen to Edward IV and her tragic sons who were lodged in the Tower and never seen again, creating a mystery which has blighted the reign of Richard III ever since;

Hostile: Wydevilles everywhere, taking over the court, having the king's ear and confidence, taking honours and positions which others thought were due to them;

Upstarts: power-hungry schemers, plotters and planners, having their hand in the effort to out-flank Richard of Gloucester and get the young Edward V to London for his coronation;

Misunderstood: in truth only obeying Edward IV's wishes and instructions. Whatever part of Edward IV's reign anyone reads, a Wydeville will be there. How they are perceived depends on the bias of the historian who is writing at that time.

Our name was written in a variety of ways: Wydvill, Wodeville, Wouldwithe, Oudeville and Wydeville. No one paid much attention to standardising words, names and spellings back then, it was an accepted fact that you could read whatever someone wrote and make sense of it without worrying about such things. We wrote with quills, a slow, laborious, tedious way of writing, not like the speed with which my words are currently being translated into 'print' on a bright screen. We just got the words down whichever way we could and if that meant taking a wild guess at the spelling of someone's name, that's what happened.

We were initially loyal Lancastrians, poor by the standards of the aristocracy of our time, rich in ambition and endlessly power hungry. There was little room in our lives for anything but the pursuance of power, without it money would be in short supply and many would go without.

We had a proud history. My grandfather, Richard Wydvill, was Esquire to the Body of the Duke of Bedford, a prestigious position that brought honours and some wealth. These positions were highly prized and coveted by many because once among the rich, famous and influential at Court, a courtier had the chance to make contacts, curry favours, carry out favours and use the influence gained to further the family's cause at all times. From this honoured position it could be seen that the family had some standing in court, or he – Grandfather - would not have been there. Where and how we gained the status does not seem to be recorded anywhere and no one said anything about it, not in my hearing anyway. Maybe an earlier Wydeville bought their way in through favours and chivalric acts of some kind or a fortunate marriage, of the kind which happened later in our family. Luck, fate, that most capricious of things, no doubt had a good deal to do with it.

What I am about to say here is background for what is to come in my life story. It took me a long time to work out the balance of power, the reason for the addiction of court life, the way to handle it. I almost came unstuck a few times, if I can use that expression in a historical book. It was not easy and took some understanding, but this is how a medieval court worked.

A court centres itself round the central figure, be that king, queen or whoever. Around the royal family are the courtiers and servants and theirs is, in truth, a tricky balancing act. Serve the king or queen with a degree of submission but not so much that the others around you notice and move in to depose you in some way. Walk the tightrope of perfect servility whilst ensuring others did not notice your attempts to curry favour. And so the velvet glove was always used: you flattered as you trod heavily on toes or apologised as you shoved someone aside, you smiled as you killed, in such a way that it looked to be the epitome of elegance on your part. Those who did not learn very quickly to be duplicitous were trodden on and thrown out with the rushes when the floors were cleared every Spring.

Court was a seething hotbed of paranoia, gossip, slander and innuendo: the trick was to sieve the information and take from it what which was truthful, ignoring the rest unless it was choice enough to be passed on to someone who would be eager to hear it. Favours for favours and they could be achieved in many ways.

It was a way of life that for some became addictive, whilst others yearned for and longed to escape to the sanctuary of their country homes where they were the lords and ladies and others deferred to them. But even away from court it was necessary to keep up standards, to follow the fashion of the day, to be abreast of the gossip – for which read slander – so you were not caught out when you went back into the hothouse once more. Everyone had their ordinary informants; those who could afford it set up an extensive spy system as well to ensure nothing escaped their attention that would damage their reputation, their wealth or their life.

Now you can begin to see what I mean. It was a very strange way of life.

Court life also meant a good deal of travelling abroad, especially to France. The marriage of John of Bedford to Anne of Burgundy was just one of the great state occasions at which a Wydeville was present: Grandfather Richard Wydvill was part of the duke's retinue of trusted friends. But there was also work to be done in England; among other honours, he held the position of Governor of the Tower of London. He had plenty to do in the service of the crown.

My father, also called Richard, was so good-looking that I heard it said some declared he was the most handsome man in England. In a time when everyone at court was handsome or beautiful, he had to be outstanding for this accolade to be given to him. We were - and are – a most handsome/good-looking family. I do wonder if some of the seemingly universal dislike of the Wydevilles stems from the jealousy our good looks, natural good manners and ability to make our way in court life generated. Just a thought.

Father too had a place in the hothouse of court, as esquire to the Duke of Bedford. This gave him considerable standing and would have made him a desirable bachelor. A man of many skills and high chivalric values, my father. He was knighted by Henry VI at Leicester in 1426 when he was just 21. He served the duke in France and thus knew, and served, the duke's second wife, the young, vibrant, beautiful, ambitious Jacquetta, Duchess of Bedford.

We were referred to as upstarts but my mother, Jacquetta of Luxemburg, was of noble descent; her father was Peter of Luxemburg, Count of St Pol and her mother was Margaret del Baizo, daughter of Francis, Duke of Andria. The addition of Luxemburg to her name indicates she was part of one of the great European families of the time. In an age where lineage, blood and property were everything, the young Jacquetta was a magnet for every bachelor who aspired to further his station in life. It was a known fact in the family that she was just seventeen when she was introduced to the Duke of Bedford, by then an elderly, lonely widower and an alliance was made which led to their marriage. This was a political move: it cemented one treaty between England and Burgundy, whilst upsetting another between England and France. In a time when treaties were regularly made and broken, this was no great surprise. My mother came to England for the first time in 1433 to secure her dower, then returned to France with her ageing husband to arrange his household to suit herself. That is not part of family lore but I know my mother...

My father, being part of the household, no doubt cast covetous eyes in the direction of the new bride, possibly envying the old man his youthful, exuberant wife. At least, that's the way I see it. I picked much of this up from overhearing the idle chatter of servants. Mother and Father never spoke of the way they met. They were just – there.

The age difference between the duke and his new wife was considerable and, as it was the duke's household, it is likely that there was not much in the way of entertainment, dances and so on, for his young duchess to enjoy. Politically it was a good marriage, but may not have been so good in terms of romance, courtship and delights. Mother did so like her gifts, her parties, her friends and – I have to say this – her intrigues.

So we have this scenario.

Richard Wydeville, my handsome father, part of the duke's household.

Jacquetta, my beautiful mother, a beautiful seventeen year old girl, ripe for romance, when she marries the ageing infirm duke.

It is not hard to envision the most handsome man in England taking every opportunity to be in the presence of the Duchess of Bedford, being of service to her, without making it too obvious.

The duke was not a well man and his health quickly declined after the wedding. He lived for a further two years, that's all. Yes, you can devise all manner of reasons why he did not last very long... and you may well be right. I am not going to speculate, not in print anyway and certainly not when my mother is around to exert her considerable influence on me, even now! After his death in 1435, Mother became one of the most desirable widows in Europe: she was not only beautiful, she was wealthy. Father was part of the escort which brought her to England to settle her late husband's affairs. I am speculating here, because I do so love a romance, that there would have been opportunities on the journey to the port, then on the seemingly endless sea journey to England, for the two young people to begin to get to know one another. Although Mother had an entourage of ladies, there were surely moments when eye contact could be made and equally it can be imagined her ladies fluttering their eyelashes and fans at the handsome knight, which would have drawn Mother's attention to him again if she had not already noticed him. He would be more than familiar to her, someone she had perhaps secretly desired but not dared to express any feelings because of her position.

No matter what preceded or indeed happened on this journey to England, the facts are that a courtship began and, love and lust overcoming common sense – when has it ever been otherwise? - they were secretly married in 1436. It had to be a secret marriage as royal permission would not have been given for someone of Mother's rank to marry someone of Father's much lower standing.

Two things come out of this: first, I reiterate that the Wydevilles were not the upstarts everyone thought we were, not a lowly penniless family dragging itself into Court by holding on to Edward's cloak as many books make out and second: it shows my parents had a love match, they knew there would be repercussions when the news broke and there were, but they went ahead anyway and the dowager Duchess of Bedford, the most desirable widow in Europe, became the wife of Sir Richard Wydeville, Knight. For that I am eternally grateful, or I would not be here and nor would all my siblings. There are those out there who will say 'good job too' but let's face it, if it wasn't the Wydevilles it would have been some other family who had a remarkably beautiful daughter of marriageable age to thrust in front of a Yorkist king who was queen-less at that time. We got 'lucky'. It happened to be us. But consider; you could be busy denigrating the name of just about any other aristocratic family of the time whom Edward had visited on his Progress around England. Now there's food for thought, which other (un)fortunate could have become involved with the Yorks and had their name go down in history as upstarts, popinjays and the like? Anyone would think we didn't work. Some of us, I would have you know, had to work damned hard for the positions we had, quite apart from walking the silken tightrope I mentioned when talking about life at Court.

Back to my life story. I love family history, don't you? Even better when it's your own parents you're writing about and you know that at least one of them is going to tell their side of the story as well. Fortunate public, getting an overload of Wydeville lives. Well overdue, I am saying as loudly as I can. Time we put our version across ourselves, rather than waiting for sympathetic historians to do it. Sad to say they are somewhat thin on the ground...

It was unfortunate that my parents had neglected to obtain the king's permission for their marriage because Father was imprisoned for a short time and ordered to pay a fine of £1,000. This was a great deal of money for a newly married knight to find. In the end a deal was struck, Cardinal Beaufort paid the fine in exchange for some of the land held by Mother. This diminished their resources a little but did at least remove the heavy burden.

The scandal surrounding their marriage rumbled on for some time but they ignored the comments and scandal-mongers and settled down to country living. It could be that the 'love story' aspect of their relationship appealed to Henry VI as he eventually took Father fully into his favour, granting him the title of Earl Rivers and then, two years later, making him a Knight of the Garter. We were pretty well on our way by then, weren't we? Edward who?

I did ask Father why he chose the name Rivers. Being a sensible, down to earth type of person as he was/is, the answer was: Rivers is a short name, no one can mangle it, no one is likely to forget it and there were no other 'Rivers' around at the time. It seemed a sensible name to take.

I guess it was. I quite liked being called Rivers, when I got to inherit the title. I just didn't appreciate the way I inherited the title, but Clarence and I have long since resolved that one between us.

Right, I've tackled a few false facts about their meeting and their marriage, now to tackle another one.

The Bury was not part of my mother's dowry.

Why anyone should think it was is beyond me. Those who said it was didn't have to look very far to find out the truth. The facts are: the land and house at Grafton was granted to the Wydevilles in 1440 by the Earl of Suffolk and his wife. So, it was not part of Mother's dowry or settlement when she became a widow. Father held land in the area, but not the actual property until this time. Is that so difficult to accept? Not that it matters, it is a comparatively trivial piece of information but it adds up when included with all the other mistakes written about us Wydevilles.

Our home was – a comforting, comfortable place bursting at the seams with children of all ages. Father was often away for long periods of time, but that didn't seem to stop the babies arriving as a legacy of each of his periods at home. Search the records if you wish, there is no word of either of them going outside their marriage vows and that is something they preached to us children, too. Vows once made were forever. Not all of us kept to that, as I will mention later, at the right time. Before you get any ideas, though, one of them was not me. I adored my wife – then and now – and had/have no intention of straying outside my vows.

Mother's marriage to the Duke of Bedford was childless. It says much about Father's virility and Mother's fertility that in all sixteen children eventually arrived and most of them survived. Being born of parents both handsome and beautiful respectively, we were good-looking and, with Mother's driving ambition and Father's contacts, went on to make very good marriages. But that was later. Much later.

A quick sideline: I've not said anywhere how I felt about my parents as people, not as aristocrats with this background or that. Behind the titles and the façade of court, they were people who laughed and cried, got sick and did all the things people do.

Father was a proud man. His loyalty to his king was total, whilst it was expedient to be loyal to a Lancastrian, anyway. When the tide turned he became a Yorkist very reluctantly and with much sorrow. His loyalty to his family came second; furthering the family's fortunes was an important aim at all times, as it was with Mother. He was a good father, ever there to listen, advise, share a jest, to bring down the wrath of Heaven on your head if you stepped out of line but he never, ever, physically punished any of us. The nursemaids and tutors had Father's permission to do that and they did, regularly. But Father never did. One of his rages was enough to stop any child in their tracks and they never ever repeated the offence. I learned from him that sometimes words are more effective than violence. Not always but often enough to validate his lesson to me. I looked up to him and followed his example throughout my life. His unfortunate end – execution after the battle of Edgecote – was a wound I carried for many years, one I believed would never heal.

Mother was revered. Mother was sharp tongued, impatient, demanding, never still, eyes, fingers and mind in every corner of the Bury, even when she wasn't there. Letters would be delivered to the house with instructions for each and every one of us. It was as if she had some scrying mirror or ball to look into, to see what each of us was doing and either praise or condemn us for it. It was frightening! We revered her and we adored her, every one of us. She was a powerhouse of energy, a never ending source of advice, wisdom and love. The more I learn of other people's lives, the more I realise how fortunate we were to have parents like this.

I need to say here that long before King Edward was a force to be reckoned with, long before the sister who would capture his heart – well, his lust anyway – got to be that beautiful, my mother was welcomed at court and was a favourite of Queen Margaret of Anjou. Mother was often at Court, where she was indulged and given jewels, where she had the ear and often the mind of many different people, where schemes were schemed and plans were planned and seeds of ambition sown which would reap us great rewards in the future. I need to say this because there are those who even now think we really did end up in Court by holding on to Edward's cloak. We were there before that. We were there as a force to be reckoned with long before the Yorks got serious about their claims to the throne, serious enough to do something about it, that is. The Wydeville side might have been considered lowborn, but Mother came from a sufficiently royal background to give her status and standing in court. We were not allowed to forget it. Our tutors and nursemaids lectured us endlessly on our position in the hierarchy of English society and what we had to do to maintain that position.

Which leads me on to another topic. Growing up.

During this period of history, most aristocratic fathers were absentees, leaving their children to be brought up by mothers, servants, nursemaids, tutors, masters and mistresses. Wives were left at home for the most part; supervising the running of the home and making the many decisions that had to be made during each day was probably the equivalent of the responsibilities held by today's young businesswomen. Money was not limitless so within a budget the lady of the manor was expected to maintain a good household, a fine board, take care of her brood of children and their education and keep the house in a state of readiness for the time when her lord was able to come home. Every tenant could and probably did come to her with their problems, whether they be health, blight on the harvest, rats attacking the stores or simply disputes with neighbours. The great festivals were occasions when the peasantry came to the house for feasts which had to be prepared, as well as a good deal of ale to be brewed. A watch had to be kept on those who 'owed' the house dues in the form of eggs, chickens, lambs or other animals. Rights were granted for young couples to be wed and build themselves a small home on the estate. The decision making would have been endless and demanding. My mother did all that, had sixteen children and still attended court. No wonder we all revered her!

On the subject of pregnancies, a well-born woman would take to the birthing chamber up to four weeks before the baby was due and would stay there for forty days after the birth, before attending the 'churching' ceremony that would allow her to resume normal life. During her time of confinement, she would be attended by her ladies, her servants and the midwife. No man was allowed into the room. Birth was very much 'women's work' with the mother-to-be relying heavily on the experience of a local midwife. Often they were highly experienced women, capable of handling emergencies but it was extremely dangerous and many women died either during or after the birth as a result of infection, blood loss or the incompetence of the midwife. Mother's successful births, despite not having 'ladies' there to support her, indicate that she was extremely healthy, had a good child-bearing body and that she had a very good midwife to attend her. There is no indication that she suffered any infection or lasting problems from the many babies. There were many families who would have been envious of such a fine healthy brood. Our reigning monarch, for one. We never thought anything of it at the time. We were just a bunch of children playing, fighting, arguing, being taught and rebelling against being taught anything that restrained us. Of course it was all needed in later life but try telling that to a three year old…

Elizabeth was the first to arrive. She was the most beautiful of all my sisters; she had a radiance that somehow shone out of her, although she had inherited a lot of Mother's tendencies, stubbornness, temper and sharp tongue.

I was next, the next son to survive, anyway. I was – and am – called Antony. Please note, there is and never has been an H in my name. No one gets that right! I like to think I was named for St Antony of Padua; lots of children were named after saints, that's if they weren't named after their godparents or parents. I quite like St Antony; he was a 'good guy' in every sense of the word. Perhaps I should have been more saintly but then I wouldn't have had as much fun, would I? The living family looks like this:

Elizabeth - Anne - Jacquetta - me - Mary - John - Lionel - Katherine - Martha - Eleanor - Margaret - Richard – Edward - Thomas - Agnes.

Every time a child arrived, a wet nurse was found immediately. Mother's role was to push the family forward at court and ensure the Wydeville line continued. This, as I have shown, she did in great style and with a regularity that many a king would have wished to emulate.

Thus, as time went on, I had many brothers and sisters to share my life.

We rose early and went to bed early, by about nine, which was early compared with people of your time where some seem to stay up all night. The standard pattern of life was to rise, to say prayers or attend the church or chapel, to wash and be dressed, to have a light breakfast and then to begin lessons, usually around six or seven in the morning. The family as a whole, whether our parents were there or not, would eat lunch together and have a large dinner in the early evening. We always had grace said before a meal and books were read to us as we ate. Us older ones acted as waiters to the adults, serving wine and certain dishes, to teach us respect for others and to be of use.

There were lessons and the obligation of church services several times a day. Whether or not our parents were there, the household continued under the direction of the Seneschal and if the instructions were to attend all the services every day that is what happened. No good any of us complaining.

Lessons were on everything from French and Latin through writing, maths and history to courtly practices, manners, dancing, music, playing instruments and composing lyrics and tunes. We had to be able to hold our own in any company any time, no matter who was there. The boys were taught to ride, to hawk, to hunt and to use a whole range of arms, from battle-axes to lances, with regular practice in the tiltyard. Armour was a way of life, we learned to wear it, walk in it, ride in it and then fight in it so it became second nature by the time we came of age. The girls were taught to ride, but their other lessons were in embroidery, sewing, cooking and household management.

It is a common mistake to think that table manners in my time were non-existent. Admit it: you thought we were all pigs at the table, didn't you? This is in part due to 'ham' acting of those taking the part of Henry VIII and other great monarchs on screen, depicted throwing bones over their shoulders and so on (I've seen some of it and laughed over it, so has Henry) and in part due to your lack of understanding of the formalities of life at that time. There is a book, "The Babees Book, Medieval Manners for the Young" which sets out in precise detail what young children should and should not do, whether it be sitting or standing in the presence of their elders, what to do if a cup of wine is offered to them to actually eating at the table, such as not leaving a knife in the trencher, which completely obviates those misconceptions. I can vouch for the book; it is absolutely right in every respect. Manners were everything: the precise form of address for everyone from the king to the tutor who saw to our education, the placing of rank at the table, who took precedence at balls and celebrations of all kind was uppermost in our training. Social gaffes did not happen; as indicated by the medieval book, respect was inculcated into us from an early age. It was a highly regulated and graceful time, with perfect behaviour demanded of all aristocratic and royal children.

We did have time for fun; it wasn't all prayers and lessons. It just felt like that when I was growing up, but looking back now, I remember spinning tops, hoops, ball games, toy soldiers, dolls and a variety of games, depending on the weather. Outside we could play rough and tumble games, inside we had to be a little more decorous, because inside we had the younger ones to consider.

Grafton was a substantial village, visited by passing traders, mummers, all manner of people coming to entertain or sell much needed items. This was of great interest to us and created high points in our lives outside the major religious festivals and the eagerly anticipated twelve days of Christmas. On a mundane level, as I said, daily life was dominated by religious devotions, just as the days of the year were dominated by the major religious festivals. Where many would perhaps pay mere lip service to their prayers and be happy to escape the rituals of the church if they could, I took my faith to heart. You will see how much when I get to my later years.

In an age when many children died at birth or soon after, to have all those living children was quite exceptional and must have been a strain on the house - and on the family finances. The considerable wealth Mother brought to the marriage mostly consisted of land on which revenues were paid. This was money not instantly available to be spent on the many people and services the household demanded. This would no doubt have made her ambitious and ever anxious for good if - not better - positions for the family.

I've been told that children of aristocrats and royalty were, as a matter of course, sent away at the age of seven to be tutored in other households. I know that's how Richard of Gloucester came to be at Middleham with Warwick, but I also know that his brother Clarence wasn't sent anywhere. So, you won't be surprised to know that my sister Elizabeth was not sent away to the Grey household at Bradgate and I was not sent anywhere to anyone at any time. Mother didn't believe in it, said the tutors at home were good enough for our family. They had to be, they had a range of ages to teach, with children arriving virtually every year or every other year, if I work the dates out in my head as best I can.

Apart from anything else, it cost money to send children away to be boarded out with someone else. There had to be at least some contribution to the care, clothing and general welfare of the child and in truth money was needed to keep up the standards that had to be maintained within the home. The women had to follow the fashions of the day, especially Mother and her eldest daughters, as they were often at Court where not to be dressed in the heights of fashion would be to draw derision from other women. The men, too, needed to be well dressed; along with the requirement to be well mounted and own both a good, serviceable suit of armour and good quality weapons. Suits of armour were expensive, as they were crafted by hand for each individual. Father and I had suits of armour and good quality weapons. The fighting men we took with us when going to battle also had to be outfitted with chain mail and weapons and some had to have horses. War is an expensive business at the best of times and the 15th century was not the best of times for conflicts. If anything was damaged in battle, it had to be repaired or replaced immediately as no one knew when the next array would go out. In the troubled times you now know as the Wars of the Roses there were many outbreaks of conflict and loyalty dictated that we responded to the call to arms with a full complement of archers and fighting men, all fully equipped and armed.

Our stables contained at least one destrier. If you don't know, this sturdy horse was especially bred for war, as it had been trained to kick, bite and generally inflict damage on the 'enemy.' Some fiction writers wrongly depict this horse as being the equivalent of a shire; it was smaller than that, with strong bones to carry the weight of a fully armoured knight and to charge into battle – or joust – as needed. Destriers were expensive to buy and so were kept for 'special' occasions, jousts, tournaments or battle. The rest of the time rounceys or coursers were used, as they were faster animals and cost less. I confess I disliked destriers; they were unpredictable animals if they had not been properly trained and you could not guarantee that. I preferred a courser every time, biddable, strong, capable of great feats of courage, never faltering when pushed into battle. You could keep your destriers as far as I was concerned.

I'm still talking money here. Wages and food for the many servants also had to be taken into consideration, along with the upkeep of the home and holdings. This would all have taken a substantial amount of money. I'm told that the quality of the education I displayed in my later life shows that I had the finest of tutors. I resented the studies at the time, despite being an exemplary student; I was fluent in several languages as my later translation work showed. Here I go again, being utterly modest and self-effacing...

I remember the family joy at the marriage of my sister Elizabeth to Sir John Grey of Bradgate. It was an arranged marriage and fortunately it was also a love match, as far as I knew. Certainly she was full of excitement and happiness at being married to Sir John, so the thought could not have been offensive or repulsive to her. The first child was taking the first step up the ladder to the higher echelons of Court.

Chapter 2 - Confrontation

All hell was breaking loose across England. Lancastrians and Yorkists were at each other's throats, literally. Skirmishes were breaking out here, there and everywhere. News arrived via an exhausted rider on a sweat soaked foam bespattered horse that the Lancastrian army had taken Ludlow, forcing the duke of York to flee to Ireland with his second eldest son. It was debated long and hard in our family whether this was good news or bad. It seemed like a Lancastrian victory in which we could rejoice but – every victory means a loser and a loser means an embittered person ready to fight back, especially when that person happens to be a Yorkist. I did not know Ludlow castle, could not imagine what wealth had been looted from there, but I did have a pang of conscience when I heard that the Duchess and her two youngest sons were captured. That I did not like. It was too close to the heart, having much younger siblings who I considered inviolate, even though I knew they were not.

There were three Earls ensconced in Calais and the orders came to remove them. Warwick, March and Salisbury were busy creating mischief over there, someone had to shift them. Orders were orders. We were on the move.

I don't know why Mother was with us that December 1459, unless it was that the Twelve Days of Christmas were approaching and she did not want to be separated from her husband at that time. Whatever the reason, Father, Mother and I, with our squires, servants and escorts, arrived in Sandwich on a bitter cold night. Father was in charge of the expedition.

Quick aside to quash yet another falsity in the history books. I, Antony Wydeville, at that time not yet knighted, was eighteen years old. I was NOT in charge of the expedition. Why would anyone think I was, when Father was still alive? Oh look, two falsities quashed in one sentence. Not bad going. I've wanted to say that for a long time and, if truth be told, this next anecdote is also one I have been longing to put right for a long time. A very long time.

I recall the cold. I recall the rutted road, the rats that fled at our approach; the dogs which snarled defiance before slinking into the darkness. I recall lights from behind shuttered windows and the sound of men at their drink. I recall feeling the sense of excitement that only being in a strange place on a cold night with the possibility of some danger ahead of us can bring. I confess that at that time I was young, innocent, untried in battle, naïve in the ways of some of the world and entirely at the mercy of what fate was to come. I recall Father looking grim but that was not unusual for him, when in charge of something, he took it all very seriously.

We were muffled up in thick felt cloaks but were cold to our bones. I know I was and there was some grumbling from the escort. We were glad to find the Inn, get the horses seen to and ourselves inside and warm and fed and then into bed.

That was our base where Father held meetings, finalised plans for the formation of the fleet, sent out messengers to instruct captains to bring their ships into the harbour ready for the great invasion of Calais. It was there we held our Christmas celebrations, ever on the lookout for anyone with Yorkist sympathies who would discover the plans.

Unfortunately, putting a fleet together is not something that can be done with any degree of secrecy. We found out later that there were many Kentish sailors prepared to slip across the channel and pour information into the ear of the Earl of Warwick in return for coins pouring into their palms. Because of this, the earl was given the task of scuppering our plans. He was a consummate sailor and knew the waters well. Whilst Father made his plans, not knowing of the spies who were busy working for the other side, the Earl of Warwick was making his plans with great care and a lot more secrecy. Information about the fleet was only travelling one way, Kent to France.

On the blustery cold day of the 15th January, the inn was shaken awake by hammering on the doors and pounding feet on the wooden stairs. We were barely given time to dress before being escorted out of the inn, through the town and onto a ship. There we were sent below decks and locked into the hold. Our squires, servants and escort were left in Sandwich. We had to hope they had the sense to at least return to Mote House and report what had happened to us. Later we discovered that John Dynham, a Yorkist, had known all along of our mission, even knowing which inn we had rented.

I had not been at sea before. It was rough, for me the journey was a nightmare of seasickness and apprehension. The ship creaked and rolled in the stormy seas, the constant crack of sails and rigging was incessant, the pounding of the waves on the hull enough to give anyone a blinding headache, without the fear that came with it. Calais was a relatively calm port in the winter storm. It was full dark by the time we arrived and our pathway to what transpired to be our temporary prison was lit by torchlight.

Now comes the part I have been waiting a lifetime (literally) to take apart.

First there is the oft-stated 'fact' that there were one hundred and sixty torches to light our pathway to the place where the Earls were staying. Who said so? I didn't count them, I know Father didn't and I am very sure that Mother didn't. She was too angry. I could feel her anger from a distance of six feet. So the first 'fact' is wrong.

Second there is the 'fact' that we were supposedly taken before the Earls and ranted at for being Lancastrian. That story did the rounds, helped on its way by the Pastons – wrongly, I have to say – and was entirely false. Someone thought it was a good idea, no doubt.

I had my revenge on one of the Pastons later on, when I had one imprisoned. Revenge definitely is a dish served cold; I am well able to vouch for that. I don't suppose for a moment the family realised why I pursued that claim for a piece of land. If they didn't, it doesn't matter. I did. But it would have been good to think they knew and were a little bit repentant. The nonsense they spread about us and this time in Calais did a lot of damage to the Wydeville reputation. It continues to this day, it was even mentioned on a Forum not so long back. I read it with incredulity. To think it is still believed, after all these years! Hard to accept, isn't it, that no one has thought it through in 550 years? No, you historians have been too busy copying from one another without using that most basic of instincts, common sense.

Back to the winter of 1460 and the rest of the slander. Oh yes, my language which was supposed to have been foul. Well, I already confessed to being an innocent. I knew curses; of course I did, having been around armourers, blacksmiths, ostlers and goodness who else, but use the language myself? Have you ever endured a whipping with a switch or, as one tutor preferred above all else, a strap? I did it once. Never, ever again. My mother was there; would I have used language in front of her? Even if she had not been, what you did not do was show your lower, rougher side to Yorkists. You maintained your dignity at all costs.

We let them talk. We said nothing. Silence is the best defence at all times. Then you cannot trip yourself up, get yourself into difficulties. I took my lead from Father and stayed silent. They said, calmly and quietly, they knew of our plans, had successfully scuppered them and that we would be held as their prisoners until such time as they decided to let us go. In deference to Mother as a woman and therefore not responsible for her actions or ours, she was allowed to leave immediately.

We were held for three months before we were able to take ship back to England.

Those three months were a turning point for me. I grew up in that time. Father and I had endless hours in which to talk or brood on our situation. We discussed land management, finances, women, court, loyalty to the crown, Mother, my future, what he expected of me, what it was like to go into battle, how it felt to kill a man and how to shut down your mind when you had done it or you would be crippled by conscience for the rest of your life. We talked of everything we could think of and still there were days of silence and bitter foreboding of what would happen to us.

Those three months were a gift to me. They coloured the remainder of my life.

Edward of March, who doubtless gloated over our predicament, had no way of knowing – until now, if he reads these words, that is – that in fact he did me a great favour. I knew far more when I emerged from his captivity than I ever did before. It hardened me and it enlightened me.

More 'facts' to be quashed. We were released before the earls invaded England in June of that year. We were not, I have to repeat this - we were not towed around the countryside as hapless prisoners of the earl of Warwick until September of that year. The earl of Warwick had far too much to do than worry about a couple of Woodvilles.

It was not a comfortable time. It was an embarrassment and a humiliation and a lesson in how to keep things secret. Bribe people more than the other side is bribing them, basically. But I would not have given up that time for anyone. It cemented the relationship between Father and me and it helped me grow up. Not everyone can say that.

Chapter 3 - Battle Lines

1460 was a bad year for the Yorks. Edward of March might have looked smug, self-satisfied, experienced and confident over there in Calais but he had two older, more experienced men to help him at the time. Clashes across the country, his father claiming the throne and not getting it, the disaster of Wakefield right after Christmas resulting in his father's and brother's heads being put on spikes outside Micklegate... I almost felt sorry for him at that time. I think I did, until the decisive battle of Mortimer's Cross, when the weather phenomenon of the parhelion – the effect of making it look as if there were three suns in the sky – gave him the chance to rally his men with the cry that God was looking down on them, there was his sign. I thought he had the luck of the devil. How many people get a parhelion when they need one, at a critical turning point in a battle, I ask you? And so the battle went to the Yorkists.

But not for long. We received the call to arms in February and went out to fight the second battle of St Albans. Yes, it was becoming a habit by then...

February 1461: cold, unpleasant weather, with snow to compound the discomfort and the problems of fighting the second battle of St Albans. We were, of course, on the Lancastrian side. The question is; what is the best weather in which to go out to actual battle for the first time in your life? What would best suit the grinding fear consuming the guts so that everything was churning and there was a desperate need to evacuate, one way or the other; the fear that you will be killed or even worse, maimed, the fear that you will be a coward in the face of the enemy and shame the name of Wydeville and Lancaster, the awful sense that you are not ready for this but there you are, riding out with a whole load of people who are grim-faced and determined and casting you sideways looks as if to assess your state of mind? I plastered on the same grim face they wore and kept my horrors to myself, as far as I could. Father understood; I had sympathetic glances from time to time but not a word passed between us. How he felt at that moment I had no idea, it was only later he told me of his own gut wrenching fear, not for himself but for his son, riding to battle for the first time. He told me that only a fool went into a battle unafraid for his life, for it was a given that they could be killed at any moment by arrow, lance, spear, sword, battle-axe or dagger. The blood lust that overtakes men in a battle cannot be denied. These were things I would discover for myself.

This was the first time my extensive training with arms would be put to the test, a time that would help me discover whether my prowess at the joust stood me in good stead when the other person was out to kill, not just unseat me from my horse. My armour was second nature to me after many jousts but the actuality of battle was something entirely new and no amount of description given by Father prepared me for it.

No one can ask for a blow by blow account of my first battle, or indeed any battle, it is too confusing. I will instead give an overall feeling, as best I can. It looks a bit like this:

Battles are noisy, bloody and frightening. Battles are a crashing conflict of senses: the overwhelming noise, horses neighing and screaming when wounded, men shouting and screaming when wounded, clash of metal on metal, bellows of encouragement, trumpeters, orders; the terrible smell of blood and other matter spilled onto the battlefield; the sights, arrows, blades, axes, lances flying, blood spattered and lethal, men's faces full of hate, destriers with huge hooves bearing down on the combatants, banners flying, badges flashing colour, the feel of the weapons in hands growing numb with exertion as man after man went down under the savage attacks. Englishman against Englishman, their loyalty defined only by the badges they wore. Every man doing his best to kill everyone who came within range, first with arrows and then fearsome weapons. Shouting men attacking others, dying men, groaning and wounded men screaming as their blood ebbed out into the field, horses charging into the massed lines, boom of cannon and clash of steel as weapons met armour or other weapons, creating a deafening, overwhelming noise. It was impossible to watch your back, your companions and your leader for signals. All you could do was keep one eye on the standard bearer, follow the flag and try to kill all who stood in front of you wearing the 'opposing' badge.

I charged in with everyone else. I swung my battle-axe against fellow Englishmen and watched them go down. I dodged sword thrusts, gave some in return. I lost my spear somewhere but retained all else, including my horse, my other weapons and my sanity. How, I do not know. I was, frankly, terrified from the moment battle was joined to the moment I realised that the Yorkists were emphatically defeated. Whether it was due to the earl of Warwick's faulty generalship or whether it was down to more effective fighting on the part of us Lancastrians is something for battle experts to argue. All that mattered to Father and me at that time was that, for once, we were on the winning side. I cannot tell you how relieved I was that Father had survived when so many had fallen. At that moment I had no relief for my safety as the excitement drained out of me. I became unutterably weary and wanted to sleep for a fortnight, a sleep in which I did not see bloodlust writ large on faces nor see the faces covered in blood as men went down under weapons and hooves. I felt sick to my stomach at the loss of men, our men, other men wearing standards and colours I knew well. I felt sadness and victory at the same time. I did not know how I felt from one moment to the next. All that was lost, though, in the sudden realisation I had survived my first battle and had not shamed myself; the Wydeville name or the Lancastrian banner.

We went home. We went home with the men who survived, looking to patch up our armour, to rest our horses and ourselves. We heard that London was in turmoil after this battle: starving, unpaid soldiers were closing in on the city whose citizens were in a state of terror for fear of being attacked and their homes looted. Mother happened to be in London: she and Lady Scales were asked by the Lord Mayor to go to St Albans and plead with the King, Queen and Prince for grace for the city. They did, with great success. This event was another gem in the Wydeville crown, Mother taking part in such a high profile mission. In court life, friendships were used for many things, not least to promote members of the family. The friendship between the Wydevilles and the Scales was to be of great benefit to me later.

The victory at St Albans turned sour for us when a messenger brought the news that Sir John Grey, Elizabeth's husband, had been killed in the fighting. There was some problem over property – whenever was there not problems over property? We were all land and power hungry at that time – and she was homeless. She returned home, bringing two small children with her. A widowed daughter to be taken care of and, what was worse, one who came with offspring. In a time when aristocratic women were there for the choosing, Mother must have despaired of arranging a 'good' marriage again for her eldest daughter.

For a time we were content to be quiet in our country home. None of us ventured out to our other homes, it was as if we had gone into shock after the battle and needed the quiet, the comfort, the security of our home where we had been so happy.

Then, on the 4th March 1461, Edward, Earl of March, was pronounced King of England.

Forgive me, I need to explore this. The gulf between Edward and I was immense, not simply because we stood on opposite sides of the political divide but because of our lives up to that time. We were the same age but many miles – if not years - apart in experience.

Edward had developed a reputation as a fearless fighter and leader, able to take on all comers and defeat them. As Earl of March he had already accumulated honours and land, wealth to support himself and those in his entourage. His father, Richard duke of York and brother Edmund, Earl of Rutland, having been killed in the battle at Wakefield, Edward had to live with the awful memory of their heads adorning spikes at Micklegate, with the added ignominy of his father's head being displayed with a paper crown, mocking his ambitions to take the throne of England. His brother Edmund was only seventeen years old when he was murdered in cold blood on the battlefield. By the time he became king, Edward had already experienced dreadful bereavement, exile and attainder and had, by his own efforts, overcome it all to march through England and take the crown both by right of accession and by strength of arm. He was a soldier king covered with glory: Mortimer's Cross was the battle that would go down in history as the one which gave the new king his 'Sunne in Splendour' standard and enhanced his reputation as a fighter and a man to look up to, a man to respect. Few dared voice a challenge to his kingship.

I, on the other hand, was still at home, helping to run the place in Mother's absence, being taught land management and farming lore, learning how to conserve and plan and rotate and do all the many things a land owner had to know. Yes, there were men to do it for you but if you did not know what to do, how could you expect to supervise others and ensure they did it right? What would happen if someone lost an entire crop you were dependent on for income? The financial side was also explained and I absorbed it all but, without a place of my own, it didn't help much. Father said I could supervise work at one of the other houses we owned but at that time we were recovering from battle, so I cannot honestly say I had hands-on practical experience at that time. I do intend this to be an honest account of my life. And so I say I was not a knight of high standing, despite the Wydeville place in court. I had fought in a battle but had also been a prisoner of the earl of Warwick. That humiliation would not easily go away. I had not lost anyone close to me in battle, I hardly knew my brother-in-law John Grey. I had not led an army to glory and on the one occasion when the new King and I met, one was captor and the other captive. There was no meeting point or common ground between us.

Some history books talk of us becoming good friends. No, we never were. We tolerated one another. I acknowledged him as my sovereign king, he acknowledged me as his brother-in-law and no more than that. He gave me honours which I had to earn; they were not given out of friendship. He was quick to scorn, at one time accusing me of cowardice when I sought permission to go on a pilgrimage rather than go to battle. He once told me I was shirking my duty to his son when I had committed hours, days, weeks to the education of the boy, spent many a long period of time at Ludlow, away from the glamour, excitement and colour of court and the translation I made of my book was for his son's edification as much as anyone else's. But I say this: Edward was generally quick to criticise and slow to praise, even with those he seemed to favour more than anyone else. He was good humoured until that person crossed him and then the humour vanished and the cold Yorkist look would appear. He liked men who were his equal. For a long time I was not able to be his equal as I had not had his opportunities. I grew up in a different world; one more cossetted and protected than his ever was. My family were ambitious but never sought the crown as the Yorks did and so we did not get involved in the bitter fighting he had to go through to get it. I sometimes wonder if he felt it was worth it. The one thing it gave him was endless access to the secret places of many women and perhaps for him that was reward enough. It was not for me.

I have just re-read that sentence. It looks as if I am saying that endless access to the secret places of many women was not reward enough for me. I have not altered the sentence, but left it there with this coda: no matter what any of the Yorks thought, I did not fraternise with women once I was married. I did not seek those secret places of women as Edward did, that part of court life was not for me. I fathered one love child. Neither of my wives gave me a legitimate heir but that did not stop me caring for them and being loyal to them. Both were love matches. Both were precious in my eyes. I have to say Elizabeth was more special – she still is – but that is the way of it, she was my first wife and so was more important to me. She gave me my title, Lord Scales, extensive land holdings, much wealth, considerable affection, all-consuming love, support and companionship. Her death from breast cancer was devastating to me.

But all of that was later, when the dust of the wars had settled and peace was made with former enemies. At that time hatred for Warwick and all Yorkist men festered in the Wydeville hearts. When the battle of Towton, that most bloody and savage of clashes, began on Palm Sunday, March 1461, we were there, fighting for Henry VI and the Lancastrian cause.

45

The weather was bitter, with snowstorms and driving winds, but it was not more bitter than the hearts of the Wydevilles. We were in full armour with our contingent of fighting men, ready to take our revenge for the humiliation of Calais. Yorkists meant Edward, Salisbury and Warwick; battle meant a chance to gain some ground in the 'one-upmanship' stakes. Whilst it was a fact of life that all knights were honour bound to respond to any call to array, no matter where or when the battle was to take place, it was also a chance to settle old scores. In the chaos of hand-to-hand fighting, who is to say who killed whom?

I have to say that Towton was an especially terrible battle in an age when battles were almost routinely fought across England. It was all the lines of men could do to hold against the onslaught, especially when snow was in their eyes and those filled with battle fever were ready and willing to take lives. We did our best to rouse the men, to keep their ardour for fighting alive and ever ready but the giant figure of Edward IV in full armour splashed with blood, his destrier covered in mud and blood, its teeth bared as he urged it forward into battle was fearful to behold and shook many a man in his boots. A skilled soldier, proficient in all aspects of hand to hand fighting, seemingly invincible, he encouraged and heartened the Yorkist men during what seemed like a lifetime of fighting.

We were in the heart of the fighting. I lost Father for a time, concentrating instead on taking as many Yorkists out as I could whilst staying alive. I know I accounted for at least ten, maybe more and the thrill I felt when they went down under the hooves and stamping feet of the armed men was like – I said that and then realised there was/is no words to describe the feeling. Exultant, triumphant, yet shocked and almost sickened at the bloodlust that was going on. We were in the thick of the fighting, if only because to do anything else would be setting a terrible example to our men and be something that would do us no favours in court in the future, no matter which way the battle went. Honour said you were in the middle of the fighting, killing as many as you could before you were killed in turn. Honour speaks out of battle time, though, honour speaks before and after the killing. Honour knows nothing of men's fever to kill and the moment that fever dies and leaves realisation in its place, the realisation that after hours, days, weeks of fighting, Lancastrians knew that the battle had been lost. Somehow you just knew it, somehow you could sense that the tide had turned and Lancastrian men were stumbling from the battlefield, were being pursued and cut down. Some were being rounded up and taken prisoner. We were rounded up and taken prisoner – again.

But we were released. For once there were no recriminations: it had been a long, proud, bloody battle with no loss of honour for the losers, just a great sorrow at the dead and wounded, the tremendous amount of dead and wounded, many of whom would not survive their terrible injuries. How Father and I got through unscathed I do not know. We were proficient fighters but we were not that battle experienced and in , anyway, it is not experience as much as luck that you evade the man coming at you with his battle axe, ready to take you down.

Truthfully, there was no shame in losing at Towton; it had been a brave fight, with victory swinging from one to the other throughout the day. It could just as easily have been a Lancastrian victory, but failure is failure, no matter how well it is wrapped up in fancy words.

We rode home to have our armour repaired, our weapons fixed, our bodies rested and our minds calmed after what was a truly frightening event. It was also a time for soul searching, to decide whether the

Lancastrian cause had any future, was it worth continuing to offer support and loyalty to a king who appeared to be losing? Would it not be a good move to declare loyalty to the Yorkist faction?

It was discussed at length in the days and weeks following the battle of Towton but only after lengthy prayer sessions and aching knees. I was more than glad to be alive and grateful beyond belief to the Lord God for watching over me during that horrendous time. Someone told me the battle lasted for ten hours. It felt like ten weeks. It felt like an eternity of noise, fear, blood, exhilaration and loss. Men I had grown up with, men who had taught me so much, were among the dead. Their teachings had helped me but their experience had not helped them. They were the unlucky ones. I mourned them as much as I would mourn a family member who had died. They were a large part of my early life and they were no longer there. I didn't expect Father to understand this when I hesitantly mentioned it to him one day but he did.

"It's like the sweating sickness or the plague," he commented, looking out of the window at the estate which was our home at Grafton. "It chooses some as victims and leaves others. Battles choose some as victims and leaves others as survivors. We were lucky."

It was only later I realised that by looking out of the window he hid his expression from me.

In June of that year King Edward, who was travelling around his kingdom, stopped at Stony Stratford, very close to Grafton. It is recorded that from there he sent a message to the Chancellor that he had pardoned Richard Wydeville, Earl Rivers. Father had made an appeal for clemency, trusting in Edward's bonhomie toward all who might be useful to him and we were able to be useful to him, of course. We had contacts, money (limited) and other assets he could call on. The appeal worked, much to our relief.

From that moment we were Yorkist in our sympathies, no matter what we held in our innermost hearts. At times you do what is expedient, don't you? Edward knew it, of course he did. It was never mentioned and in view of what happened later, he probably managed to bury the thought that we once fought against him. It would have been good had his brother Richard done the same thing, but still... in this life you can't have everything, much as everyone would like to.

For a time life was normal, as normal as it gets when you are the siblings of a mother once highly regarded at court and who regretted and resented her loss of power and prestige. She made up for it by making our lives hell in her drive to make perfect courtiers out of all of us...

I had things to do and I did them. And so that moves me on to my next subject.

One question keeps coming up in reference to me – my daughter Margaret. I have to confront this, even though I would like to avoid it, as it is a deeply personal matter and I dislike bringing it to the fore. But... she is a living fact of my life and it needs must be spoken of.

For the record, Margaret was born before my marriage to Elizabeth Scales. I met Gwenllian Stradling at a reception at one of the Wydeville homes, which one I now disremember, and fell in lust with her. No other word for it. She was beautiful and charming, talented and intellectual, everything I wanted in a woman. I courted her for a while but it became clear that the family were not interested in a marriage between a Stradling and a Wydeville, for whatever reason. It also became clear that she was not as interested in me as I was in her, so in many respects it was a fortunate thing that the marriage could not be arranged. It would have been a disaster. But, Gwenllian was – shall I say – free with her favours where I was concerned, in part in rebellion against a strait-laced family who wanted to keep her locked up all the time and in part because of her own sensuality which was quite overwhelming. The result was a child. She was named Margaret after my sister, a name we both liked.

The family was livid. So was mine; actually. My mother was not happy with me at all; thinking I was tying myself down to some chit of a girl who was unsuitable for the ever-ambitious Wydevilles but calmed down a good deal when she knew there would be no marriage. The Stradlings were not entirely happy but a generous payment to them for the upkeep and maintenance of the child quietened much of their ire.

It wasn't long after we 'converted' to the Yorkist cause that Mother arranged an introduction for me to Elizabeth Scales, widow, daughter of Thomas, 7th Lord Scales. Mother told me she was pretty (she was), amenable (she was, very) had money (enough to keep me happy) and that all round, it was a good match. What Mother didn't take into account at the time was the instant attraction between Elizabeth and myself. It was a spark that flared into a conflagration which did not go out for many years. But more of that as it seems appropriate. Mother disdained the word 'love' whilst admitting she lived only for her husband, her man, all the rest of us were supposed to have dynastic marriages to carry the Wydevilles on to fame and fortune. We weren't supposed to fall in love. As far as I was concerned, a marriage without love was not worth having. That was a result of growing up in a household where parents were so obviously in love. Blame Mother…

And so, just one year later, with Lancastrian uprisings still ineffectually flaring up around the country, I obtained the king's permission to marry Elizabeth, Baroness Scales.

We had a subdued but well attended ceremony at Middleton Hall in Norfolk, the family seat. Many local dignitaries came, many Wydevilles came. It was a quiet and pleasant day when I was legally bound to the woman I had come to love in the intervening period. And don't let anyone tell you otherwise. Stories abound that the Wydevilles led Edward astray, contributed to his hedonistic lifestyle, were rampant around his court (and I mean that in every sense of the word) of which about half could be said to be true and even that is stretching the truth somewhat. It is part of the 'Wydeville slander' to blame his downfall in health on us. I was married, I honoured the vows I made; so did Elizabeth.

For the record, and it needs to be said to ensure there is no slanderous talk anywhere about my child, my wife knew of her, we visited her together and we talked of her to others. When it became clear that our marriage would not produce a child of our own, Margaret became more special and I sent money regularly to help the family look after her.

I took my seat in Parliament as Lord Scales. This I did in on January 28th 1461, along with Warwick's brother John who had been made Lord Montagu, Humphrey Bourgchier who had been made Lord Cromwell and Lord Fitzwalter. High ranking aristocrats with whom to share the Parliamentary sessions. I felt honoured and at the same time the equal of them. Rank came easy to me, as easy as putting on a cloak. I could walk and talk the part without thinking about it. Lord Scales. It suited me. I was prepared to be Lord Scales for a long time.

A quick aside here to quash yet another comment raised in a respected academic journal. I did not need to have my seat in Parliament ratified when I became 2nd Earl Rivers; I already held the right of a seat in

Parliament by virtue of being Lord Scales. If the person(s) who query that care to take it further, I suggest they consult Debretts, which is what happened earlier, before this became my book and not a formal biography. The original book contained that information. It has been checked. The person who said I was not entitled to enter Parliament as Earl Rivers was, as so many are and continue to be, wrong.

That same year my sister Jacquetta was also married and became Baroness Strange. Two fledglings had left the Grafton home for good lives in high society. Mother said she was well pleased.

For a time.

Chapter 4 - Changes

At this point of my story I was just twenty years old. I had followed Father's example and excelled at jousts. I had gone with Father to Sandwich and there found myself captured on the orders of the Yorks and imprisoned for some time. I fought at the battle of St Albans and again at Towton, that bloody and appalling battle that took so many lives, once more finding myself, albeit briefly, a prisoner of the Yorks. I had seemingly made a good enough show of my conversion to the Yorkist movement to appease the new king, in that I had gained permission to marry a wealthy widow and take on the elevated title of Lord Scales and Newcelles as well as inherit a good deal of land around the country. I had taken my seat in Parliament as a lord of the land. I was with the King at the siege of Alnwick Castle. I was a rising star.

Court was becoming a place where I could negotiate the quicksand of politics with some skill, only getting my foot caught in the sand once or twice and quickly extricating it when I realised I was in danger of sinking. I was able to observe Richard of Gloucester, someone as different from King Edward as it was possible to be. Gloucester seemed to me to be an introspective man, observant, sharply critical, of few words but of considerable power. I summed him up in my head in one word: dangerous.

I liked George, duke of Clarence. He seemed my type of man, someone who enjoyed his position in court, liked fine clothes, good jewellery, had an eye for quality horseflesh and enjoyed his food and drink. Sometimes a little too much, I have to say, but every man has his weakness and surely they are permitted that. Clarence played an active part in the great tournament which I will speak of later. He helped a good deal with the arrangements and had excellent ideas when it came to putting on an ostentatious display. He said it was all the more enjoyable for not being his money he was spending...

I saw a good deal of Warwick, too. A big man in every sense, power sitting on his shoulders like an ermine cloak. He carried a persona somehow that meant when he walked in a room, everyone knew he was there even if they didn't turn round to see who had arrived. Mostly they did. Many courted him for his attention, his largesse, his influence, to see how it could benefit them. I deduced he knew this and played them at their own game. I also deduced he thought he 'owned' the new King and I knew, somehow, he was wrong and he would find out how wrong he was in the future. Little did I guess at that moment how Warwick would be proved wrong, never dreaming of the future elevation of our family. I had limited psychic powers which I used to good effect most of the time, but such a vision eluded me.

Mostly, though, I was enjoying married life and familiarising myself with my new possessions.

Our first home was Newcelles Manor (also known as Newsells as well as a variety of other spellings but I prefer Newcelles), a beautiful, elegant house set in substantial grounds near Royston in the county of Hertford, just north of the village of Barkway. The print which exists does not show the house I lived in. That was an amazing house with great sweeping wings and a soaring portico. For your information, the property came into the Scales' family in 1255, when Peter de Rochester granted Newcelles Manor to his sister Alice, widow of Robert de Scales. It devolved through the family until the property, together with Middleton Hall, with its great hall of plaster and framework, beams and black oak carvings, Sandringham in Norfolk, a most beautiful estate and house, Mote House in Kent, properties in Cambridgeshire and other counties, became part of the Scales' inheritance and gave us newly-weds plenty of scope for travelling the country, visiting our many estates.

It was after surveying all that I then owned that I tried for the piece of land in Norfolk belonging to the Pastons. It was a deliberate move on my part; I harboured resentment against the Pastons for their slanderous, scandalous story about the capture of Father and myself. I would not – could not - allow it to go unpunished. So, when someone told me that John Paston might not be freeborn and therefore not entitled to own land… it was a gift to someone who was seeking revenge. I had the king's ear and 'justice' was quickly brought to bear. It mattered little to me whether I acquired the land or not, all I wanted was the Pastons put down by Lord Scales. As I said earlier, whether they ever made the connection between my desire for the land and their scurrilous letters, I have no way of knowing. It matters not at this distance of time, but it mattered then. You did not cross me at any time and get away with it.

For the next two years, life was relatively quiet for us; there were no upheavals in our day to day living. I was enjoying being a land-owning magnate and busy working at establishing my presence at court. As a former Lancastrian, I had ground to gain and maintain. Allegiances were easily broken if you were not sharper than the next courtier; if you did not keep an eye to the main chance of keeping in with the reigning monarch, no matter what private thoughts you might hold about him.

Then my sister Elizabeth met Edward – and life stood on its head. There is a story, so 'well documented' that people believe it to this day, that she sat under a tree with her two small sons, awaiting the King who was on a hunt. She was planning to play the maiden in distress and get his attention. Yes, well, any sensible woman would do that, wouldn't they? Keep two small boys under control whilst waiting possibly hours for a king to come riding in... There is even a print of the tree, would you believe...

Actually they met at a reception for Edward in one of the great homes in the area, to which she was fortunate enough to be invited. My sister was and is a stunningly beautiful woman. Edward ever had an eye for a lovely face, which she has, combined with silver-gold hair which streams down to her waist and beyond. I rarely saw that hair let down but when I did it was amazing.

They saw one another as often as they could, as often as his commitments would let him, that is, and we were all sworn to secrecy. Somehow we kept it secret too, in part because to say anything would have jeopardised the family's one huge chance at – success, fame, fortune, wealth, positions, marriages, you name it we would have lost it. No way were we going to do that!

And so the year 1464 goes down in history as the turning point for the fortunes of many people, not least the Wydevilles. In the May of that year, in secret, the king of England married a Lancastrian widow with two small sons. She just happened to be a Wydeville. And she just happened to be pregnant.

Edward could never stay out of a beautiful woman's bed. Believe me, I know it well, saw it many times. "Come To Bed" eyes doesn't really sum it up. He had an animal sexual magnetism that mesmerised virtually every female he looked at. My sister was no different. So they bedded, she got pregnant and he decided he wanted to marry her.

What he did not need, or want, was a child conceived before marriage. There was enough talk when the marriage was announced anyway, which he knew, without there being a pre-wedding child to complicate the issue. But he was equally determined no one else would have her, so – he married her and kept her shut away for the remaining five months of the pregnancy.

Meantime we knew, but didn't mention, that the Earl of Warwick had 'plans' for his protégé and we knew but didn't mention that the Earl of Warwick would be mightily displeased when he found out that there was a binding marriage which prevented his protégé from marrying some European princess and creating a dynasty that would have better suited the Earl. We have to be honest here, all right, I have to be honest here, Warwick wanted Edward to marry someone that suited him, not someone who suited Edward. This is probably why he went ahead and married someone of his choosing, rather than anyone else's. If nothing else, Edward was ever his own man.

For Jacquetta, dowager Duchess of Bedford, wife to Richard Wydeville, Esquire, this had to be the crowning achievement of her career in court. I often mused on how Mother felt when it happened. What did she think when she stood there and watched her daughter married to the King of England? Her daughter to be queen of England. It was a dream come true, if she ever dared dream such a thing. That too I often muse on, Mother has never said.

We were all bound to keep it secret. Apart from anything else, Edward was almost as devious as his brother Richard in his dealings with the court and parliament. Child aside, as it were, he held the news back until precisely the right moment, when he could throw it into a council meeting and watch the disorder which broke out.

The child, a boy, was quietly taken away and brought up in some aristocratic family. So, the books may say my sister bore her husband the king ten children. She did, ten 'legitimate' children – but we all know what happened there, eventually – whereas in truth there were eleven. Where that other one went, what happened to him is anyone's guess. It is a sadness to me that there is a nephew somewhere I never got the chance to know. I have no doubt he grew up handsome and intelligent, a combination of Edward and Elizabeth would have ensured that.

There was a delightful sense of smugness and anticipation for us Wydevilles during those endless weeks. The 'I know something you don't' feeling kept deep inside. Courtiers were very sharp at picking up nuances. Little did people know that insults, sarcastic comments, snide asides, aspersions cast on any Wydeville were being noted, marked down in a mental notebook, awaiting the day when every person who had said anything out of place would have to retract it.

It also gave us time to come to terms with the new honours we had to accord to one of our own. From aristocracy to royalty is a very large leap indeed.

My sister was older than me by some five years but, apart from her time as wife of Lord Grey, we had grown up together, ridden together, broken bread together and attended Mass together. We had studied under the same tutors and suffered the same punishments for slothfulness, lack of attention, lack of respect and many other naturally childish transgressions.

That companion, that sibling, had overnight taken on the mantle of the highest honour in the land. In essence, my role had changed from being Lord Scales, magnate and land-owner, to humble subject to my own sister. I had to kneel, remove my bonnet and accord her the title Your Grace every time I met with her. The familiar face had to become unfamiliar, had to be treated with such deference and reverence that all would know I honoured the Queen of England.

How did that feel to a proud aristocrat? It is surprising that no one has asked this question in any of the books. I was delighted, overwhelmingly pleased that my family should be so honoured, that we had the high standing in the land Mother had long fought for in every corner of court. But another part of me resented the bended knee, the doffing of caps or bonnets, the deep bows I had to make before someone I had once run with, fought with, played with and prayed with. It wasn't easy, no matter how you look at it.

If I might quote from the medieval report written at the time of the tournament which I fought with the Bastard of Burgundy,

'As he left Mass, he went close to the Queen of England and of France and Lady of Ireland, his sovereign lady, to which he was a right humble subject. And as he spoke to her ladyship on his knees, the bonnet from his head as he should, her ladies clustered around him.'

The point here is that I declared myself to be 'a right humble subject' of my sovereign lady. But you see; our upbringing had inculcated into my psyche the need to be deferential to all who ranked higher than me, no matter who they were. Even though I thought: 'this is my sister and here I am, on my knees before her, bare-headed and dutiful and I feel I should be able to stand up and speak to her, face to face' I could not do it.

As with so many dry-as-dust academic books, most historians are concerned with the events of the time, rather than the personalities of the time. They don't seem to want to understand – or are incapable of understanding - that personalities create actions, motives create forces which, once set in motion, are difficult to control. Every aspect of a person's character can - and often does - dictate their actions which in turn often provoke great events. Yet they – historians - persist in ignoring it. They rarely speculate. Somehow they never consider us as living breathing loving hurting human beings. If they did, someone would surely have asked how it felt when a member of our family became Royal.

Maybe one day someone will explore how the Spencers really felt when Diana became Royal.

My sister's elevated status did mean I got to spend considerably more time at Court, associating with my new brother-in-law. You will recall I already said that some books claim we became good friends. No. Toleration at best, no more than that. Edward, it seemed to me, wanted the woman but not the family and found, to his irritation, it didn't work like that. Brides come with family, in our case, a lot of them.

On surface we presented a united front to the court, but behind the smiles, no one knew what thoughts really went on. We were good at dissimulation, we had to be: it was part of the great game of court life. It meant going as far as ensuring that, if possible, even your eyes did not display your true feelings to another for fear of character (or financial or even real) assassination. The smallest slip, the most innocuous comment delivered to the wrong person could lead to a fall from favour and consequently removal from the riches that could be found by simply being there, being friends with the right person or being in the right place to overhear this piece of gossip or that snippet of valuable information.

One comment was made about me that I wish to quash right now. An historian said that I did not leave as much of a mark on history as I could have done. That was because I knew well how to play the game: be charming but not as charming as my monarch, show intelligence but not to the level of those above me in the ranking at court, be pious but not to a degree that would upstage leading churchmen and be chivalrous, but not to the degree that I would outshine other, older knights and aristocrats. The perfect diplomat.

And yet Edward saw something in me, something that he may have considered a threat in some way, for the honours given to me later in life seemed designed to ensure that I was kept away from court: Lieutenant of

Calais, Lordship of the Isle of Wight and Governor-guardian to the young Prince of Wales. This last prestigious position required me to live in Ludlow. Each of these posts was a great honour but each carried that underlying theme: my being away from London and away from court. The choice of honours bestowed say a great deal about our relationship. We tolerated one another because Edward could not be seen to snub his brother-in-law and I could not do anything but be deferential to my sovereign lord because without Edward's patronage, I would not be able to increase my wealth and lands. Not quite a Mutual Admiration Society but a working relationship that was part of the courtly Game of Life as lived at that time. The great gulf between us had simply grown greater: Edward the revered soldier-king, I merely an aristocrat who happened to be the brother of his Queen. Memories lingered of the shambolic and humiliating incident in Calais and later the capture of Father and me at Towton. The memories continued to rankle as there was no way vengeance could be taken for the insults given at the time of capture. Whilst there was no 'rant', enough was said to make it clear we were considered beneath them. You do not easily absorb that and forgive. Honour really demanded restitution of some kind; but the mere fact Edward had, of necessity, to honour me as brother to his Queen was sufficient revenge and that in itself was a source of quiet satisfaction to me and the family. Apart from Mother, who had claims to European society ancestry, we were upstarts in the eyes of the court. But we were upstarts who had to be taken seriously, for we were entitled to honours, influential marriages, wealth and positions in court.

It is not difficult to picture my sister asking for high ranking marriages for the family and picture Edward in conference with his closest advisors, working out the best way to deal with this influx of new people: marry this one off to this person, placate another with a position there that would enable them to accrue wealth and as for the brother, well, there were many positions, honourable ones, which would keep him out of London and out of the Court. She has never said, she is too diplomatic for that, but I would place a very large bet with whoever would take it that is precisely what happened. I know my sister...

Did I dislike my honours? No. I had a good life. I had a seat in parliament and a place in court; I had many estates and much to do. I never went anywhere without a large retinue surrounding me, just because I could. Whichever way I looked at it, Edward IV marrying Elizabeth Wydeville had done us all a huge favour and in the light of that, I guess it was not really so difficult to go to my knees and doff my cap to the new Queen.

I need to say I realised that all this was a world away from the peasantry whose toil supported the aristocrats; in essence 95% of the population were toiling to support 5% of the population. I never lost sight of that 95%. I was welcomed by all everywhere I went, all right, I am about to be modest again... this was in part due to my charm and in part to my ability to speak easily with people on all levels of life. I was, in many ways, the perfect diplomat, in court and in life outside, in the 'real' world. And so I survived more years than others did in positions of high authority and great wealth, I played the court game to my advantage and won more times than I lost. I did lose a few times, Lieutenant of Calais was lost to me, for one, dashing off into exile with Edward, a foolish thing to do but it seemed like a good idea at that time, was another... but on the whole, I won more than I lost. Until the end. I leave it to you to decide, when we get there, whether the game really was worth the candle.

Chapter 5 - The Emprise Begins

Court life had settled down by Easter of 1465. The King's marriage seemed to have been accepted, Wydeville alliances and positions had been arranged - if reluctantly in some quarters – and everyone appeared to be happy. It was a time of quiet in what was normally a turbulent world. It seemed it was time to throw a bit of excitement into court life. I assure you I had no idea what my sister was planning, scheming, call it what you will. Forgive me if I spend a little time on this part of my story: it is an aspect of court life that is not mentioned very often – the tournament is but not the ritual leading up to it - and it meant a great deal to me. It also goes to show you how ritualistic our life was, not to mention expensive. It seemed money was endless and we could do with it as we wished. So we did.

After the Easter Mass, I went to find my sister, to ask her how she was spending her day and to take her my Easter gift. I had a pendant in my pouch which I had arranged to be made for her. As I walked along the corridor towards her rooms, I saw her coming, surrounded by her ladies. As I had to, I went down on my knees and swept my new bonnet from my head. Her ladies fluttered around me like a swarm of beautiful butterflies, all silks, satins and lace and I felt something, fingers and coldness, and looked down to see a gold collar, set with gems, fastened around my right thigh. Hanging from it was a 'flower of souvenance', which translates as remembrance. This is a sign which indicates an emprise, simply, a chivalric adventure, an undertaking.

The collar itself was extremely expensive. It was solid gold with many precious gems set into it in a design that was both intricate and unusual. It was worthy of being an emprise, it really was that special.

The 'flower' hanging from it was a small gold perfectly formed lily. The beauty of the thing was breath-taking.

I got up and went to thank them for the great honour. It will be hard for you, in your time, to appreciate the magnitude of the gift. The challenge to take part in an emprise is not given lightly. The one throwing down the challenge has to know that the person who is being challenged is a fit and likely candidate for it, that they have not only the money – these things were invariably extremely expensive – but had the courage and stamina to see it through. My sister knew me well enough to know I would accept, no matter what it was.

I was still holding my bonnet at this time, not being able to replace it on my head until my queen left my presence, as it were. She began to move away, her ladies fluttering after her. In the excitement of the moment I had forgotten her pendant. Recalling it, I started to go after her but then I looked in my bonnet and saw a small scroll tied with gold thread.

There were 'rules' to the setting up of an emprise. The whole event was set about with ritual which added to the romantic chivalric aspects. Ritual was an integral part of our life then, far more than now. The nearest equivalent I can give you is the spectacle of the Trooping of the Colour, that sedate, precise ceremony which is ringed with ritual. An emprise went far, far beyond that; it was almost the stuff of which myths are made. It was as if much had been inherited from King Arthur's mythical chivalric knights. My sister knew the rules well, knew that it would set the Court by its ears to have such a thing set on its way, would give plenty of tongues plenty to talk about. She played the court game as well as I did.

I stood there, holding the scroll, thinking it through. Elizabeth had spent a lot of time working on this emprise. First she had to come up with the theme; then she had to arrange for the collar to be made, not an easy task. The court jeweller would have been summoned, the drawings shown, the practicalities worked out and finally a cost agreed. I shudder even now to think what it had cost her. Or Edward. No doubt he had been in on the planning, it bore all the hallmarks of a soldier king wanting to regain a little of the thrill of battle.

Once the collar had been made and delivered – I do not know to this day how they knew the right size unless they bribed my tailor to give them the exact dimensions of my hose – the wording had to be composed for the scroll, which contained the actual challenge. Then it had to be written out and tied with gold thread in a very elaborate way, closed with Elizabeth's personal seal. After that, she and her ladies schemed how to 'present' me with the challenge. What better time than the Easter Mass? She knew I was likely to have an Easter gift for her, knew I would have to go down on one knee to her, knew I would remove my bonnet... they were all given their roles and they played them to perfection.

I knew full well what the rules were and how to follow them, so rather than open the scroll myself and read the terms of the emprise, I took it to Edward and asked him to break the seal and read it. That was important; I needed the king's permission to take part in whatever it was the ladies and his Queen had requested, if not actually ordered, me to do.

He was surrounded by acolytes, hangers-on, if you like, when I found him and handed him the scroll, with the request he open it and reveal the contents. The fact there was not so much as a raised eyebrow told me he knew what it contained. With great ceremony he broke the thread and handed the scroll over to a courtier to read aloud to all who were there.

I was not entirely surprised at the contents: the challenge was to set up a tournament. I was commanded to appear in the City on a date and at a time to be set, with a preliminary date of October that year, to fight a joust with a noble knight. We were to fight on horseback, armed only with spears, then go to swords, the number of strokes to be limited between us. I had to deliver spears and swords to my opponent so he had the choice of which we would use. It was agreed that if one of us were knocked from their horse, without the horse falling as well, it would be held that the fight had ended. If either was hurt by spear or sword and could not carry on, it would be held that the fight had ended.

The tournament was to go into a second day when the combatants would fight on foot with spears, axes and daggers. If we chose, we could carry shields. The rules permitted one throw of a spear, after which we would fight with the other weapons. All arms were to be presented to the noble knight so he could choose and, in the event of no agreement being reached, the king was to be the arbiter. The cost of transporting the knight to the tournament would be borne by me. Simple enough yet complex enough to involve hours, days if not weeks of planning, decision making, letter writing, commanding… just as an emprise should be. In every way it was perfect. A chivalric adventure, a great spectacle, an honourable undertaking. I was thrilled.

The costs eventually proved to be substantial, as the knight I chose to be my challenger brought with him close on one thousand men and many horses, not to mention his entourage of servants and all his possessions. They had to be transported, housed, fed and cared for in every way… it just went on and on. There were times when I cursed my sister for involving me in the undertaking, at other times I revelled in the planning and the anticipation of the great event.

The first thing I had to do was choose my opponent. After a lot of thought and discarding a lot of names, I chose Sir Anton, the Bastard of Burgundy, Earl of Roche and Lord of Bever and Beveresse. I knew the knight's reputation well, knew of his fighting skills and valour.

He would be a worthy opponent. It had to be good, or it would not have been real, can you understand that? A lot of money was going to be spent; we had to put on a decent show, not a half decent one. No mock fighting, no faking the blows – despite what some historians, one in particular, said about the tournament. Believe me, I was there. I know how much I was bruised when the fight was over – she wasn't. Wydeville bias again, even though that comment was made in a book about a Wydeville, my sister. Obviously the historian had no time for me. Nothing unusual there then.

Having made the decision, I had to write to Lord Anton. This I did and then asked Chester Herald to make the journey to Europe and deliver the letter. More elaborate arrangements, it wasn't as simple as my writing a letter and he going there and delivering it. He had to take the collar with him to prove the emprise and so even this part of the chivalric adventure was wrapped around in ritual.

The Earl of Worcester, Constable of England at that time, was commanded to record the memorable act so that it would be remembered. The collar and flower of souvenance then became generally referred to as 'the emprise', an item in itself. It was in turn a token; a contract and a challenge, all in one golden collar and flower. Elaborate rituals indeed.

The rest I had to learn by hearsay, of course. As far as I know, it was at the end of April when Chester Herald arrived in Brussels and, from his lodgings, sent a letter to Lord Anton that he was newly arrived from England with a licence from me, then Lord Scales. Lord Anton sent two heralds and two messengers to Chester Herald to accompany him to the duke's home. There Chester Herald presented his credentials, including the letter from me, which Lord Anton accepted, leaving the Herald to return to his lodgings while the letter and credentials were considered.

At the beginning of May, the commandment went out that all the heralds and messengers in the Burgundian court should go to Chester Herald's lodging and bring him, in style, to Lord Anton and the duke of Burgundy.

After a good deal of ceremonial speechmaking, (we were exceptionally good at that in our time) Chester Herald went into a side room where he donned a surcoat displaying my coat of arms. Then, with the emprise carried on high on a silk kerchief, covered modestly with the cloth, he returned to the main audience chamber, bowing three times as he approached the duke and Lord Anton. After bowing for the third time, he uncovered the emprise and displayed it to the gathering. As he stood holding it, another noble knight read my letter aloud to everyone. Sir Anton approached the duke and asked for permission to touch the emprise and accept the challenge. Having obtained that agreement, he then went to Chester Herald and lightly touched the collar. He made his acceptance speech and then, with great ceremony, the emprise was covered again with its cloth. The cloth and its precious contents were then left in a side chamber.

Next morning Lord Anton informed Chester Herald that he could not give a full answer immediately, as he had to confer with the duke. He asked the Herald to be patient. This was something Chester Herald was more than happy to do as he was, in effect, on holiday. In all, he waited nine days before he was summoned once again to the Court, there to receive a letter to take back to England, accepting the challenge. He was given a rich gown ornamented with sables, the very one the Knight was wearing at the ceremony of the touching of the emprise. It was extremely valuable. He was also given a pouch of money and his costs for staying in Brussels were refunded. That was a help, the emprise was already running away with my money... Chester Herald was then escorted in great style some distance out of Brussels to start his journey back to England.

It was not until the 23rd May that the Herald finally arrived back at Greenwich. There he related in detail everything that had happened, advising Edward, myself and all the rest of us who were there, the duke of Gloucester, the earl of Worcester and others, of the gifts he had been given. Honour, it would seem, had been seen to be done on all sides. Chester Herald was happy, he had valuable gifts and his name had been recorded for posterity as the bearer of the letter. The emprise, the challenge, was set. All it needed was the right conditions, a serious amount of planning, a good deal of money and London would have a spectacle indeed.

It sounded exciting. It was exciting, but it would be two years and more before my opponent arrived in England to complete the emprise. A few things got in the way, a war or two... which preoccupied him during that time. I was fortunate not to lose my challenger to injury or death during that time, or the whole ritual would have had to start over again with someone else. I spent some of that time discussing tournaments and their management with my father, who in 1440 had fought a big showy tournament with Peter de Vasques of Aragon. First-hand experience of such events is hard to come by. I made the most of my opportunity.

Meantime, those of us in England had other things to think about.

Chapter 6 - Coronation

The marriage of Edward IV and Elizabeth Wydeville may have seemed like the pinnacle of fame and fortune for the family in Mother's eyes but the Coronation was to seal our family's status once and for all. With such an accolade for his Queen, Edward was promoting her - and the entire Wydeville family - to a very high level, that is, above the rest of the court. No one dared say a word about the 'upstart Wydevilles' in our hearing. I don't know how she cajoled Edward into giving her the Coronation, I didn't ask and I wouldn't ask even now, some things are too personal, but she did it.

Having been unable to stage the great tournament and complete the emprise, thus giving Londoners a state occasion to talk about, a Coronation was a suitable alternative. It also has to be remembered that England – London in particular - had been denied a great wedding. This was a reasonable alternative and meant a good deal to the new Queen. Whether this adequately compensated for a hushed hurried marriage, though, is anyone's guess. I believe she would have liked a big wedding, with glittering ceremony and loads of guests; most women do, it would seem. My wife wanted a reasonably small wedding as it was her second time, but we did invite a lot of people and it was a lovely occasion. Elizabeth's was a secretive affair held in deepest darkest Northamptonshire… not quite the thing for a King and a new Queen, I would have thought, but still… Edward did what Edward wanted to do. I wonder if the Coronation was his payback for that, in a manner of speaking. I never did raise the question with him.

The Coronation was held on Ascension Day, 26th May 1465 and was an expensive, showy affair. First there was the ceremony of appointing new Knights of the Bath, traditionally held at the Tower. Then there were very elaborate pageants and processions, all very secular until the Queen entered Westminster, then the religious aspect took over. London was decorated as only London can decorate itself for such an occasion, with huge 'sculptures', arches, flowers, dignitaries, you name it they did it.

I've read a report that a group of Luxembourgers arrived at Ship's Green and made their way to the Abbey, carrying shields on which were painted images of Melusine, the water-witch. The face of the witch had been deliberately designed to resemble the about-to-be-crowned Queen. This apparently set off 'witchcraft' rumours around the Abbey, which it was designed to do. It is said that I drove them out of the Abbey and back to Ship's Green, where I refused to allow any of them to embark until I had faced each one in hand-to-hand combat and scratched the image of the 'witch' on their shields.

I need to say first:

Our mother was descended from the Luxemburg royal line, so is it likely that Luxembourgers would resent her daughter being crowned Queen of England? Apart from any other consideration, my sister Elizabeth had by that time been Queen for a year and three weeks, thus giving plenty of time for anyone to register their disapproval of a Wydeville being elevated to the highest position in the land. Many questions hang over this report, such as why they should go to the trouble of hiring a ship to take them to England for that occasion when, as has been indicated, she had been Queen for some time and there had been many other occasions on which a protest could have been made, (albeit a Coronation is a very high profile event), why 'witchcraft' should be brought into the equation by people from a country far away from England, in both physical and historical terms and why I should have gone to the trouble of fighting them one at a time before sending them back on the ship. I had a Coronation to attend, surely the best thing would have been to drive them all back on ship by ordering my guards to do it, rather than waste all that time, energy and the possibility of damaging a good sword, by doing it myself.

The second thing is this: it's a load of ********. Enough said, I think.

Referring to witchcraft, though, I have to mention that on the 10th February 1470 Mother was formally accused of witchcraft, of using her arts to entice the King's affections towards her daughter. It did seem that the court couldn't accept that Edward had chosen a commoner, a Lancastrian widow with two small sons, to be his consort. They were desperately looking for a reason outside the simple fact that Edward had been attracted by her outstanding beauty. A beautiful woman surely does not need witchcraft to ensnare a man. Nothing was proved and the court had to go on enduring us en masse in their midst, whether they liked it or not.

I was Cup-bearer at my sister's magnificent Coronation, part of the glittering ceremony and the feasting which went on afterwards. A day of pride and gratitude. Pride that this was the seal on the rise of the Wydevilles, gratitude to Edward, my sovereign lord, for arranging such an elaborate ceremony. We had a wonderful time, all of us. Edward didn't attend, at that time kings didn't go to the coronation of their queens; don't ask me why, it was just a tradition. He got drunk with his friends and courtiers who were not invited. I think I got the better part of the deal, even if it was once again hedged around with ritual and a good deal of having-to-be-nice-to-people-who-resented-the-Wydevilles action. I was getting good at that.

Nothing changes. I want to include here, if you will forgive me, the fact that my sister's coronation ceremony was identical to the one your current queen starred in all those years back. History doesn't just repeat itself, history is all around us and we are all a part of it, whether we like to think that way or not. 500 years apart, two identical ceremonies for two Elizabeths.

Chapter 7 - Court Life

As a good Queen should, Elizabeth produced the first child of their marriage nine months after her Coronation. Her daughter Elizabeth arrived on the 11th February 1466. No doubt Edward would have preferred a son but a living child was something to be celebrated. He seemed delighted with his daughter and went around giving honours to people, along with considerable amounts of ale. I became Treasurer of England. This high rank was a great honour and increased my wealth quite considerably.

By then I'd again written to Lord Anton, enquiring when the emprise could be completed. It was surely time for the great tournament to take place.

My sister was pregnant with her second child when the emprise at last got under way. A Queen capable of conceiving so easily was something every king craved; it seemed Edward IV had chosen well as far as that was concerned, although the court was still very much against us. My emprise was an attempt in part to show the aristocracy what my family was capable of. I knew that the reputation of the Wydevilles – and the Scales family, come to that – rested on my shoulders. I had to do well in the tournament, I had to win or the 'disgrace' would add to the calumny already being heaped on our heads. It was very much a case of 'how the Wydevilles were trying to be more than they actually were with such an elaborate occasion.' It mattered little that the King had gone along with it – provided I met the costs, of course.

I mentioned the cost before.

It went something like this:

Transport for the noble knight and his entourage, his lodgings and accommodation for all who came with him together with stabling for the horses.

Great banquets in his honour.

Certain roads in the City of London to be sealed off in order to accommodate the tournament, that had to be paid for. (For which read bribes, of course. We were going about the king's business at that time; it should have been enough for anyone. 'Would you please ensure that this road and that leading into the City and in particular those around Smithfield are closed to all comers on the day we specify.' 'Right, sire,' would come the answer, 'we'll do what we can.' But drop coins into open hands and it becomes 'the roads will be closed, sire.' No question of it. The way of the world, then and now, it would seem.)

There was the cost of building the barriers, the staging, the pavilions for Lord Anton and myself and all the other accoutrements for the actual joust.

Money for the men at arms who would be present on the day, as it was an exceptional occasion.

Money for the heralds. Money for the people at the gate. Money for -

Then there was the show I had to put on. I couldn't just ride in and start the tournament. Nothing as simple as that. It had to be showy; it had to be expensively showy.

New weapons had to be provided and I had to have a new suit of armour for the occasion, too.

At times I began to believe the emprise would bankrupt me, but I got through. Just.

The planning was a joint thing. We didn't quite form a committee but put together a working team of Sir John Tiptoft, Earl of Worcester, a man I much admired, the Earl Marshall, the duke of Clarence, who loved such big state occasions, myself and a few others and we began the work. Edward had a major part to play, too, as he too loved ceremonial, especially when it meant a contest like this.

The lodgings for Lord Anton and his many men were organised, even though at that time we had no idea how many were coming over with him. Orders went out that on the dates, which we would supply later, this banquet and that would be prepared – my chef took over then and wrote out the menus so everyone knew in advance what was needed. Along with the money, of course… The Inns of Court were told, by order of the King, that they each had to provide four men-at-arms as part of the King's guard when he went to Smithfield for the tournament. Word came back, privately, that they were not best pleased about this but there was nothing they could do about it. A royal order is a royal order.

Carpenters and others were advised, no, make that ordered, to build the barriers and the stands. I chose the colours for my pavilion and directed they use Lord Anton's colours for his. Orders went out for the new weapons and I was measured for a new suit of armour, as well as new clothes for my Grand Entrance on both days. There was No Way I would turn up in second hand armour, even if it was my own.

It was all very time consuming and I had to leave my wife to take care of the estates whilst I worked on all this, which was far more important, of course. She was more than capable of taking care of any disputes, problems, accidents or otherwise in any of our homes. I had every confidence in her and she in turn had every confidence in me that I would stage the most incredible tournament imaginable and that a great light would shine on the name of Scales. With that kind of backing I was prepared to do just about anything to make it happen, for her sake as well as mine.

It seemed as if we worked up to the last moment, but looking back on it, there was time to relax. I was at Greenwich for some time, awaiting Lord Anton's arrival. I had a whole group of people with me; we whiled away the time playing Tables, cards and other games. Hard life, I know… but I couldn't leave London in case Lord Anton arrived. My wife came to Greenwich a few days before Lord Anton came, able to give me the good news that nothing major had happened during my absence and that she had dealt with everything that needed dealing with. I told her then, as I told her many times during our marriage, I had every confidence in her and she was the finest wife any man could want. She still is.

John Smert, Garter King of Arms, remained at Gravesend for the entire time I was at Greenwich. He had the job of welcoming Lord Anton and escorting him to London. His lodging had to be paid for…

On the 29th May word went out that - at last - Lord Anton was arriving. It seemed he had been delayed by this and that, mostly inclement weather but at last he was there. As planned, when Lord Anton's ship neared the English coast, John Smert boarded a barge and sailed out to meet him. They made contact about two miles off shore and Lord Anton was given the formal greetings of the King and his court. His ship moored up overnight and he sailed up river to Black Wall on the 30th May. There he was met by the Earl of Worcester and many high-ranking dignitaries; so many that they needed seven barges and a galley to accommodate them all. Each barge and the galley were decorated with rich tapestries and cloth of gold. We were all set to make as big a display of ostentatious wealth as humanly possible. Did someone mention money for this show?

After another official welcome, Lord Anton was escorted to St Katherine's Dock, where he boarded one of the official barges and was taken to Billingsgate, where there were yet more people to welcome him, mostly officials from the City. I have no idea what he thought of all this, I guess he accepted it as his right. A superb stallion was waiting for him at Billingsgate (from my stables, I might add) and he was escorted in great style through Cornhill and Chepe, past St Paul's and finally to the Bishop's Palace in Fleet Street. It was Edward's idea to lodge Lord Anton there, in a suite of rooms hung with tapestries and cloth of gold. Nothing had been overlooked; everything was sumptuous elegance and comfort. Then we could really get things moving; orders went out for the banquets to be prepared for Lord Anton and his entourage. He had a secret place to practice before the tournament, too. I was too busy with preparations to take time out and practice; I had to hope I was in good enough condition generally to make a fight of it.

A barge was placed at his disposal as well as his ship if he wanted to use it. He had everything he wanted during his stay in England. The tournament was as much a diplomatic event as a chivalric one: Edward wanted to show the court of Burgundy he knew how to stage a great event and shower honours and respect on the contestant we had chosen.

Up to that time I had not met my 'friend', although I knew of his reputation. I was anxious to assess his physical presence, but could not be seen to be anxious. I had to hold back my impatience and play the Court game. Waiting.

Edward arrived in London on the 2nd June. He had ridden from Kingston-on-Thames with an entourage of princes, dukes, earls, barons, knights, squires, the mayor, aldermen, sheriffs and commoners of the City, kings of arms, heralds and messengers, you cannot believe how many tagged on to make it a stunning procession. The Constable was carrying his baton, the Earl Marshall was there and between them was Lord Scales, the man himself, carrying the king's sword. This was IT, in a manner of speaking. I Had Arrived. All the rest of it was incidental; this really was IT, riding into London at the head of a procession of how many people? Couldn't count them. I was in royal blue slashed with silver, heavy with gems, a great silver chain round my neck with a huge sapphire as a pendant, rings on most of my fingers. The ones on the fingers holding the king's sword were especially large. Of course. I'm sure most of the light shining in London that day was the sunlight glinting off my teeth as I showed the biggest grin in the world. Take that, London: Antony Wydeville, Lord Scales of Newcelles, had arrived. And how!

At the city walls Edward (for which read me as well) was met by another massive group of dignitaries, priests, clerks and others who formed into yet another procession as we made our way to St Paul's. There, mitred bishops with incense were waiting to receive him and guide him to the high altar where he made his offering. I got a chance to say a few prayers too. I felt I needed them. After this, the entire group rode to Fleet Street where Lord Anton was waiting with his entourage around him. The colour, the noise, the splendid display of so many richly attired high-ranking people was a magnificent start to the whole emprise, giving Londoners a hint of what was to come.

I had my first sight of my opponent as I rode into Fleet Street with Edward. In rapid succession I thought: a worthy opponent indeed, I chose well. I can win against this man, even though he looks to be a man of skills. He is a champion in his own right, I will need all my fighting skills... he was broad of shoulder, looked strong in the arms, had a determined look about his eyes and was a true knight. He sat his horse better than many men I had known – jousted, that is – and I was aware that even as I assessed his strengths and looked for his weaknesses, he was doing the same to me. I would not have expected him to do otherwise. We exchanged greetings with a hearty handclasp that showed his strength but which I withstood. He was a worthy contender. I was well pleased with my choice.

From Fleet Street the whole procession moved on to Westminster, so that Edward could begin his parliament the next morning.

On the 3rd June Lord Anton appeared before Edward, asking that the day of battle be fixed. I am not sure if he was impatient to be smashed to pieces by me, or just playing the courtly game. I tend to think it was the latter. My father put the same request on my behalf, both saying that it should be as soon as it pleased the king to arrange it. I certainly was impatient to smash the great Lord to pieces; I had a lot of accumulated anger to work off. On the surface life was wonderful, beneath the surface all manner of rumours, innuendos, sly looks and the occasional bitchy comment told me that the Wydevilles were a long way from being accepted. It brought what I considered to be natural anger and I had to work it off somehow. How better than a one to one 'battle' with a first class opponent? I had to hope he wasn't carrying as much anger as me, or I might get more than I bargained for.

Edward called his counsellors and commanded that the Sheriff of London should begin work on the field at Smithfield. The Constable advised the Sheriff to call the King of Arms to arrange this and for the field to be made firm and stable. This was a formality, much of the work had already been put in hand; it was too big an undertaking to be done in a week. If the stand collapsed with the king in it... or the London dignitaries, or the ladies... so, much preparatory work was already under way. It just needed the actual date of the tournament for the work to speed up. That date was Thursday 11th June. Edward immediately postponed his parliament from the Wednesday to the following Monday. A tournament was much more interesting than a parliament and no doubt there was little that was so pressing it could not wait a few days.

When all this was done, I rode back to Greenwich, where my wife was waiting for me. I had much to tell her and much to arrange, trivial details such as what to wear when entering London for such a ceremonial occasion, for example. My Elizabeth was good at things like that.

On Friday 5th June I travelled into the City aboard my personal elaborately decorated barge. I have to confess the barge was a particular pleasure. We all had them, but most people treated them the way they treated a carriage or a fine horse. I loved travelling on the Thames, loved the movement of the barge, the river traffic, the whole scene from start to finish. Descending the steps to board the vessel was a thrill every time. I never got used to it, never took it for granted. I was wearing a long gown of gold cloth and a lot of heavy gold jewellery as well. It was not a time for modesty. The barge moored up at St Katherine's and I was received by the Constable, Marshall and many other dignitaries who then travelled with me through London, all of us on horseback. A herald and a messenger bearing my coat of arms rode before me. In great style, then, I was escorted to the Bishop's Palace of Ely in Holborn where I stayed in apartments hung with tapestries of silk and cloth of gold. The ceremonials didn't include women, unfortunately. I would have been even prouder if my wife had been able to be on the barge with me. To ensure her comfort, I arranged for the vessel to return to Greenwhich and collect her, so she could join me later in the Bishop's Palace. My armour, weapons, clothes, horses and attendants were already in London, close by. I had nothing to worry about except the tournament itself.

As far as I was concerned, the first part of the emprise was complete; both combatants were in London, one resting from his journey across the water from

Europe, the other from his journey up the Thames to London. Both had been ceremonially greeted by most of London's high ranking officials, both were staying in elaborately decorated, beautiful rooms with every possible need attended to.

The second part of the emprise was about to begin.

Chapter 8 - The Tournament

Nothing could be hurried or rushed when it came to the emprise. Rules and conditions had to be discussed at length so that all parties were satisfied with what was going to happen. A meeting was arranged at St Paul's where the minute details of the tournament were gone over by the counsellors for both of us.

I had Earl Douglas, Sir John Asteley and Sir Laurence Rayneforde as my counsellors.

Lord Anton had Sir Simon de la Layne, Mons. G Launde de Tholongeon, Mons. Petre de Wassue, Mons. Philip Cohane, Mons. Phillippe Bastard de Braban, Mons, Moferent, Mons. Foresters, Thomyson Dore as his counsellors. He would have more than me, wouldn't he?

The two groups were in separate inns, with messengers, squires or pages, scurrying back and forth with the various points up for discussion. Everything had to be right before either of the contestants set foot on the field of 'battle'. God forefend if anything went wrong... I was there with my counsellors, all of us reclining on settles and/or comfortable chairs, clutching ever full cups of fine wine, endlessly discussing each point raised by Lord Anton's counsellors. This went on for some days, as there was much to be considered and agreed upon. A fraught time, as you can imagine...

The first point to be discussed was whether there were any doubts over the conditions set out by me in my letter. Was there anything which Lord Anton found objectionable? The answer was no but a clause was inserted into the conditions: it was agreed that no harness fitted with long daggers of any kind would be allowed on the field. Sensible. Neither of us wanted the contest to be over before it started.

The second point was what was meant by 'one of us be borne to the ground' – as in, was it that the hand, the knee or the whole body should be brought to the ground, or one of them. These were serious matters and open to all manner of interpretation. My advisers settled for one or the other of them being brought to the ground, rather than any one part of the body. I was prepared to go along with whatever they decided. It didn't matter to me, I had no intention of being borne to the ground by him, or anyone, come to that.

The question of spear throwing was brought up for discussion: it was agreed before the Constable by both of us that we should cast our spear only, not use it for any other defence.

There was a clause in the rules which said that we would run at each other on horseback with spears and then set to with swords. The question was asked, if any of the horses were struck by either of us to the extent that the horse did not live, did that mean the tournament was over? It was agreed that neither us intended to hurt the horses and that if the unfortunate event occurred, we could change to another horse and continue with the tournament.

It was also agreed that should either of us drop our sword during the run at one another, if the king so commanded, the sword would be given back to whoever dropped it. Another point was agreed, both of us should have someone to help charge their spears, if we wished.

It was decided that after the spears and swords were delivered to Lord Anton for him to choose, he should make his choice in his own time. That one baffled me. What else could we do but wait for him to make his choice? Strange, but they wanted it in the conditions, so it went in the conditions.

Another point arose over the eventuality of one or other of us being knocked out of the saddle without the horse being brought down as well; could it be said that the tournament was over? Lord Anton's counsellors requested that the king should make that decision. That seemed fair to me. After all, I had no intention of being knocked out of the saddle any more than I would allow myself to be borne to the ground. I had no intention of losing this tournament, whatever it cost me to survive and be judged the winner, that I would do.

They also wanted to discuss the question of whether either of us would ride a horse which would fight or bite. Lord Anton's counsellors said he never intended to ride such an animal in the tournament. My counsellors said for my part I did not intend to take advantage by means of horse, but to use my hands and skills with arms. Lord Anton didn't know I had an aversion to destriers and would not have used one in the contest even if it were available.

Then the counsellors came up with another point, if either of us should lose our sword in the combat, would it be lawful for that person to lay hands on his opponent by the neck or anywhere else. This matter was brought before the Constable of England and eventually it was agreed that either contestant might take advantage with hand or sword as he desired.

After all this was done, the formal command went out to finish the field and sand it as appropriate.

Things were moving - at last.

As I said, the work for the great day had been going on for some time. The field had been prepared strictly according to Edward's instructions. The lists had been made; they were one hundred and twenty yards in length, ten foot, eight yards in breadth and ten foot, double barred. There was a full five foot between the barres. The cost of that alone was two hundred marks. I know I keep saying it, but it was a very expensive occasion... even for me.

There was a fine lodge for the king on one side of the field, with steps to the high platform where a seat had been arranged for him; seats and stands were ranged below it on three levels for other dignitaries and important people. There was a matching, lower stand on the other side, specifically for the Mayor of London and other dignitaries, Aldermen and lawyers. There were galleries for the ladies, too.

There were two pavilions for us contestants, one at each end. Mine was of double blue and tawny satin, embroidered with my letters. It was made up of seven panels with many banners displaying my coat of arms and the addition of a valance of crimson cloth of gold. Rather elegant, I thought. Lord Anton's pavilion was equally richly decorated, made of white and purple damask with a gold pommel, the valance of the tent being made of green velvet embroidered with his motto, NULL 'NE CY FRETE.

A St George's banner was fixed in the posts of the lists beside the king's tent on the right hand side, with a further fifteen banners set in posts around the field. They made it look festive and decorative and fluttered madly in the summer breeze.

The day of the contest dawned bright and clear. Any threat of rain, as we had seen in the days before, had blown away overnight. I looked out of the window of the Bishop's Palace at the blue skies over London and smiled. It was going to be good. Messengers came to tell me that there were many spectators gathered outside the field in West Smithfield, together with food vendors, street criers, entertainers and no doubt a few pickpockets and other villains, too. They were waiting to watch the arrival of their king, his many followers and all the high ranking officials of London as well as the contestants. And every one of them, I knew, would be trying to outdo everyone else with elaborate clothes.

My wife travelled early to Smithfield with an armed escort so she could take her place in the ladies gallery before I arrived. Then, about an hour before the tournament was due to start, I rode from the Palace to Smithfield, surrounded by my armed escort and followed by my elaborately decorated string of horses. That was good, riding into the City with my procession. I could see by people's faces it was impressive. I had to hope it was as good, if not better, than Lord Anton's procession. Nothing had been said but we both knew how to play the game, we both knew what spectacle we had to stage.

Outside the field I met the people who would head my procession and we swiftly organised ourselves. It had been arranged that the duke of Clarence would carry my helm, so that was handed over to him. I warned him not to drop it... The earl of Arundel, the earl of Kent, Lord Harry of Buckingham, Lord Herberd and Lord Stafford were each carrying one of the weapons we were offering to Lord Anton for the 'fight'. This was done in a few moments and then we entered the field.

I recall each of them was wearing doublets of vivid colours, stiff with jewels and I was wearing silver slashed with purple for the first day's events. My horse was draped in white cloth of gold, with a cross of St George made of crimson velvet imposed on it. It was bordered with a fringe of gold a full six inches long. I was followed by nine other horses, all elaborately and beautifully decorated. The second horse was draped in velvet tawny, decorated with many great bells. The third horse was draped in russet damask down to its hooves, decorated with the two letters of my device done in gold. The fourth horse was draped in purple damask reinforced with gold work, bordered with blue cloth of gold and at least six inches of thick braid. The fifth horse was draped in blue velvet, made with pleats of crimson satin along the drape, also decorated with gold. It had a border of velvet on green with more gold. The sixth horse was draped in a cloth of crimson gold, edged with fine sables and bordered with eighteen inches of sable. The seventh horse was draped in green damask to its hooves, also decorated with gold and bordered with russet cloth of gold to a depth of at least six inches. The eighth horse was draped in tawny damask. The ninth horse was draped in ermines, bordered with crimson velvet and adorned with tassels of gold.

Riding each of these horses was a page from my household, wearing a mantle of green velvet embroidered with gold. The sun shone on this extravagant display, the gold thread, tassels and fringes moving as the horses walked, sending light in all directions. I can tell you I had a wonderful time arranging all this, drawing horse after horse on sheets of vellum and deciding how each one would be decorated. Elizabeth had her input on that, too. I hoped it measured up to her expectations. I was looking for her as I rode in but there were so many ladies crammed into the gallery I couldn't pick her out at first.

Edward was in purple, that I did see and I also noticed that his counsellors were all white headed men. Someone said it looked rather like a Roman senate, a king and his wise, wise men. They were right. But the counsellors were not there for wisdom; they were there for a contest. Below Edward were knights displaying their heraldic devices, then Archers of the Crown, each holding a pike which glittered in the sunshine. Below them was the Earl of Worcester in his role as Constable of England along with the Marshall of England, both wearing elaborate robes. They had their seats from which they were able to issue orders relating to the proceedings.

My wife told me later how the Mayor and Aldermen of the City of London had arrived, preceded by a sword carrier, who had turned the point of the sword down as they bowed and then knelt before

Edward and then took their places in their stand. She told me about the eight men at arms, weapons glittering, mounted on fine horses that entered the field and waited to receive orders from the Constable.

You can read all this in the official report as it were, the one written at the time, if you want. I'm remembering how I saw it, how my wife saw it and the rest is in the report. But then again, by now you should be taking my word for what happened, after all, I was there, and you need not bother with a difficult-to-read report. Not difficult for me, I'm at home with that 'antiquated' language but I know full well you're not.

Satisfied that all was as I had arranged for it to be, I rode forward, sitting tall and proud in the saddle, for after all this was my day and I was there at the direct command of my Queen. I presented myself to the Constable, who asked why I had come. I declared loudly it was to accomplish and perform the Acts set out in the letter sent by me to Lord Anton, the Bastard of Burgundy. Edward, having had confirmation of this from the Constable, commanded me to enter the field. I dismounted before Edward and, surrounded by noble lords, made my obeisance.

The excitement surged through me as I made my triumphant, elegant and showy entrance to the field. All eyes were on me and my entourage: I had arranged for every page to be properly dressed, tried to ensure that every horse would behave itself by choosing only placid mounts, that nothing would happen to disrupt the show I was staging for the benefit of Edward, my sister and most if not all of the dignitaries of London who had come to watch. The emprise was my sister's idea and I had worked hard to try and ensure it was carried through without a hitch. There was always the chance of something unexpected happening, a horse being spooked and throwing its rider, one of the weapons being dropped, just about anything. Human frailties come into every great venture, but the first part went without a hitch. There were great sighs of relief and a large amount of self-satisfaction that The Arrival had gone so well.

When everyone had been given sufficient time to admire the wonderful display I had created, as arranged, I had the horses taken out of the field to make room for my contestant to enter and went to my pavilion to wait for the moment of 'battle.' I had carefully sited my pavilion in such a way that I was able to watch Lord Anton ride in and see what kind of elaborate entrance he made, without making it obvious that I was doing so. He would have known, of course, he would have done the same thing had our situations been reversed. As I said, we both knew how to play the Court game.

And I waited in great anticipation and some trepidation, I have to say. It was not a battle, I wasn't in danger of being killed but I could be hurt if I didn't manage to evade my opponent's spear when we rode at one another. The honour of the Scales family and even more, of the Wydevilles, was in my hands that day. My armour was put on as I awaited my opponent's arrival. That in itself sent anticipatory thrills through me. The moment of 'conflict' was fast approaching.

The roar of the crowd outside and the excited voices in the field told me that Lord Anton had arrived. I recognised the duke of Southwark carrying Lord Anton's helmet. My opponent had an entourage of nobles and counsellors and a procession of twelve beautifully decorated horses. It was a truly elaborate display of ostentatious wealth. His horse was draped in crimson garnished with long swaying silver bells, a stunning sight. The second horse was led in by four knights wearing drapes of his coat of arms. The third horse was draped in ermines to its hooves and wore reins of fine sables. The fourth horse was equipped with leather armour (cour boullie, leather which had been boiled to soften it and then shaped to make the bardes, plates, of armour) and draped in cloth of gold. The fifth horse was draped in crimson velvet which had been decorated with a device of eyes full of tears, all in gold. That was slightly creepy, I thought. The sixth horse was covered in cloth of silver right down to its feet. The seventh horse was draped in green velvet covered in gems. That must have cost a fortune, I thought. The eighth horse was draped in fine sables down to its feet, with reins of ermine and so it went on. It almost outdid my display, suffering only slightly from being second. The crowd had already seen my display; he just had more horses than I did. His pages were dressed in violet gowns, ornamented with two white pleats and one yellow pleat, garnished with gold. It was impressive; I had to admit that. He had obviously spent as much time drawing horses as I had.

Lord Anton went through the ritual of demanding the right from the porters to enter the field. Having been formally allowed in, he approached Edward and said (as far as I can remember):

"Right high, right mighty and right excellent Prince, I am come here before your presence as my judge in this party to accomplish and fulfil the acts of arms conveyed in certain chapters sent to me by Lord Scales, under the seal of his arms, that is here." Well, it was something like that. The usual hyperbole, anyway.

I knew the procedure. Edward would say 'yes' and indicate that the tournament could begin. He would be anticipating a good show and I wanted to ensure he got one. I had the distinct feeling that he was half hoping I would fail. I can't say where I got that from, but I was rarely wrong on such things.

Lord Anton retired to his pavilion to have his armour put on whilst the swords and spears were presented to Edward, who approved them. Then both counsellors were summoned and the spears and swords were taken to Lord Anton so that he could choose his weapons, as we agreed. The spectators were by then anticipating a really good day of knightly skills.

Whilst all the presentations and preparations were going on, heralds went to the four corners of the field to blow their horns, get everyone's attention and make their proclamation. This I can repeat from what was written at the time. Someone wrote it down because they had to be word perfect and so they read from their scripts:

"And so it is that the most Christian and victorious prince our liege lord Edward IV by the grace of God king of England and of France and Lord of Ireland, has licensed and admitted the right noble and worshipful lords and knights, the Lord Scales and of Newcelles, brother to the most high and excellent princess the Queen our sovereign lady, and the Bastard of Burgundy, Earl of Roche and lord of Bevere and Beveresse, to furnish certain deeds of arms such as be comprised in certain articles delivered unto his highness by the said Bastard, sealed by the said Lord Scales with the seal of his arms, for the augmentation of martial discipline and knightly honour, necessary for the tuition of the Catholic faith against heretics and miscreants and to the defence of the right of kings and princes and their public estates, for so much we charge and command you, on behalf of our most dread Sovereign Lord here present and on my lords the Constable and Marshall that no manner of man of what estate degree or condition he be of, approach the lists, save such as be assigned, nor make any noise, murmur or shout or any other manner token or sign whereby the said right noble and worshipful lords and knights which this day so do their arms within these lists or either of them shall move, be troubled or comforted, upon pain of imprisonment and fine and ransom at the king's will."

Now you see why it was written down. No one could remember all that and get it right.

I've put it out in full for one reason: so you have an idea of the whole courtly culture this emprise came from and was built on. It had to be like that, it was part of the Court game. Nothing trivial, nothing incidental, this was full blown ritual with neither of us able to change one part of it to suit ourselves, even if we had wanted to.

Lord Anton, having chosen his weapons, came out of his pavilion and mounted his horse. I came out, mounted my horse, cantered over and we took our places at each end of the lists. The moment I had been waiting for had arrived: the tournament began.

I really need you to picture this. I was taking part in it, so I can only give my impressions but the overall picture is exciting, two closely matched knights charging at each other, hooves pounding on the sanded earth, sunlight glittering on the armour and long sharp spears, manoeuvring for a chance to strike - but neither of us was hit. We paused at the end of the run, turned and faced one another. The spectators were silent; it was almost as if they were all holding their breath. My man was standing waiting; I handed him my spear and began to strip off some of the armour to give me freedom to move properly. It seemed Lord Anton had the same idea as he began to remove his armour at exactly the same moment.

We rode back, met about half way down the lists and began to fight with swords, filling the arena with the clang of metal on metal. I had to watch him; he was a sharp and skilful fighter, especially at close quarters. My horse was obediently responding to my every nudge but his was beginning to be restless. Suddenly its head shot up and toward me, then it reared back with a scream of pain and before I knew it, horse and rider were on the ground. I heard the great roar that went up from the spectators and above it I heard Edward's fearsome loud voice yelling "Foul!"

I spun my horse round, holding my sword aloft to show I was taking no further part in the fight at that moment and spurred the animal over to the stand where Edward was shaking his fist at me. I dismounted and, without a word, snatched the trapping from the horse to show my saddle was strictly within the parameters set down for this tournament. Seeing that, Edward sat down again without another word. I could not read his expression; his face was unusually blank, as if he was deliberately masking his thoughts but again I had a good idea what he was thinking, that I was determined to win by any means. He was wrong. Very wrong.

By the time this had been done, Lord Anton was on his feet and his attendants brought him before Edward. The rules of the tournament permitted him to have another horse brought onto the field but he declined and we were ordered by Edward to return to our pavilions. It transpired, after the stewards had consulted and looked and poked and prodded, that it had been an unfortunate accident, the result of Lord Anton's horse striking its nostril on a projection on my saddle. The pain had caused it to rear up and then crash to the ground. It had died immediately and in doing so, had trapped its rider beneath it, which was why Lord Anton had been unable to get up.

My man told me that when he reached his pavilion, Lord Anton said: "doubt not: he has fought a beast today and tomorrow he shall fight a man." That was a slight exaggeration on his part but he could be forgiven, it had been a humiliating accident. I felt deeply for him, it had been his big day and his horse had let him down. We relied heavily on our horses, buying only the very best. He had ridden a thoroughbred, heavily armoured as it happened; yet an unfortunate accident on the horse's part had resulted in a nasty tumble and the death of a fine animal.

The Constable came to tell me Lord Anton had decided not to fight on that day. That was fine by me, I had done my chivalric best, given a good display, ridden a good joust, even if it had ended rather abruptly and I knew I had scored points in the sword fight. The Constable had visited Lord Anton's pavilion to ask if he was wounded or hurt in any way. He apparently said he had no wound and he would be ready to fight on foot the following day, provided the king gave him permission to do so. It was likely that the fall winded him badly and he did not feel capable of putting up a good fight. Nothing was said about wounded pride, but it was not for a chivalrous knight to admit to such a thing.

I got rid of the rest of my armour and went to sit in the stands near Edward to watch the remainder of the jousts. There were plenty of knights ready to do 'battle' and entertain the spectators. I had the next day to look forward to, a chance to really show what I could do. In the meantime I could relax.

I caught sight of my dear wife in the Ladies Gallery and sent her a quick smile. We did nothing as common as wave at one another even though I wanted to, but she knew she had been acknowledged, her vivid smile back told me that. Nothing was said by anyone sitting close to me, but they all knew full well of my great love for my wife and she for me, so they should not have been surprised at the communication between us. Court conventions or not, we always acknowledged one another on these occasions.

Day two of the tournament promised to be an exciting one. A joust was always worth watching but hand to hand fighting between two well-matched knights was a better spectacle by far.

Edward arrived in style again; accompanied by his large retinue and by my sister who was anxious to see the emprise through to its climax. Edward took his seat, looking relaxed and remarkably regal. I make that comment because, despite his imposing height, his ability to wear a doublet with great aplomb and to make a heavy cloak look like the lightest thing ever created for a man to wear, somehow the crown, the whole 'royal' bit, never sat truly easy on Edward's head. It was as if he was perpetually about to launch into an attack, a physical one, that is, not a spoken one. Edward, so much the soldier king, was seemingly never entirely comfortable with the trappings of being a monarch. He was too active, too physical a man, if I can say that. But this second day he looked regal, calm, expectant; his purple robe genuinely flattering him. I doubt he would appreciate my comments, but on second thoughts, perhaps he would, he knows his fighting prowess was second to none and he knows too that he loved to be in action, hunting, hawking, dancing, yes, womanising, too, we all knew that. It was as if he had too much energy even for his large frame and remember, he was a giant among men at that time.

I waited outside, hidden from view, as he had to make his grand entrance first. When all the dignitaries were once again in their stand and the chattering fluttering ladies were in their gallery, I rode in. I was already in full armour, apart from my helmet which once again was carried (carefully) by the duke of Clarence. This time my horse was draped in crimson velvet with thick embroidery depicting my coat of arms and was fringed with gold. Following me onto the field were seven horses, each with a page as a rider, all wearing rich clothes decorated with gold. I was accompanied as before by the Earl of Arundel, the Earl of Kent, Lord Harry of Buckingham, M. Bouirghchier, Lord Herberd and Lord Stafford, each of them carrying one of the arms for the day's contest. These were two casting spears, two axes and two daggers. My other seven horses were all decorated, but I won't bore you with the details, it is sufficient to say they were as glorious as the horses I had led in on the first day and I had spent as long designing their trappings as I had all the others. Yes, we covered a lot of parchment drawing the outline of horses and then working out what each one would wear to make a fantastic display. My wife was imaginative in the extreme and we had some wonderful designs made up. This display was as much her doing as mine. I just paid for it... After all, the entire emprise was a spectacle for not only Edward's pleasure but the standing of the Scales/Wydeville family as well. Reputation and honour was at stake. I knew it and accepted the responsibility for it.

In a repeat of the day before, the Constable demanded to know what business I had on the field and I in turn declared I had come to perform my arms on foot in accordance with the articles I had sent to the noble knight Lord Anton of Bever and Beveresse. Permission was given; I rode onto the field and dismounted before Edward to make my humble reverence to my sovereign lord. Then I went to my pavilion to await my opponent.

Lord Anton arrived, accompanied by the Duke of Suffolk, the Earl of Shrewsbury, Lord Mountjoy, Sir Thomas Montgomery and others. He too was asked why he was there and declared that he had come to perform his arms on foot in accordance with the articles sent to him by Lord Scales. He too made his humble obeisance to Edward and then retired to his pavilion to await the start of the contest. Ritual, always the ritual. Once that had been done, we could get down to business.

My man kept me informed of what was going on. He stood in the doorway of the pavilion, saying things like: "weapons going to the King, sire. He's handling the casting spears; don't look like he cares for them too much. No. He says this is an act of pleasure – is it, sire? – and you can't use them. I did think they was a bit dangerous, sire, didn't you? Looks like daggers and axes going to the Bastard."

That suited me. I preferred close quarters fighting rather than with casting spears, more chance to make an impact, as it were. I sat in my pavilion, pretending I was not in the least bit excited, nervous; anxious or any other emotion about the fight to come. I was, but I dared not give away the merest hint of nerves. It was not the done thing.

I heard the heralds make their proclamation to the gathered spectators, then the Constable visited my pavilion to find out if I was ready for the contest. I told him I was. He went to Lord Anton's pavilion to find out if he too was ready. When all had been checked with the King of Arms, Edward ordered the cry of 'lesses alers' to be called and did I not think the moment would ever come? I came out from my pavilion carrying my battle-axe. Lord Anton came out of his pavilion and, right in front of Edward, we began our contest.

I remember this as if it were yesterday, not 542 years ago (as at the date of writing this, anyway). It was one of the most exciting and challenging moments of my life and I had a few of them…

Anton stalked toward me so I began to move toward him, switching my battle-axe from shoulder to shoulder and then hand to hand. It was all show, of course. I could feel the nerves twitching and jumping and knew I had to make a move, because the moment the fight began, all nerves would go. It was this pacing toward one another nonsense, this 'show' bit which got to me. If this had been a real battle, I would have downed him by then, or he would have had me on the ground, suffocating in the mud. Instead we were playacting, at least at first. It soon changed, though.

I aimed for his visor with the head of the axe, at the same moment he aimed at my breast-plate. He must have decided the same moment as me that we had to get going; all else was a game. And then, with the nerves gone, we began a serious fight. Don't ask me to give you a blow by blow description, all I know is we fought one another as if we were in a real battle. I recall the clash of metal on metal, the ringing sound in my ears from the many blows to my armour, the sense of being battered and giving as good as I got. I am saying this in detail because I want to repeat that at least one historian, dare I say a foolish one? all right, I will, it is my book after all, at least one foolish historian had the blatant nerve to say that the fight was stopped by Edward after two or three blows had been exchanged. Madam, I can assure you that if you had done your research properly - and it is not difficult in this day of Internet and goodness knows what else to call on - you would have found the reports of the fight and the damage done to both our suits of armour. That would have told you what a tremendous fight we had.

There is also the fact that Londoners talked about the fight for years afterwards. Believe me, it was a fight. Believe me, I was bruised and battered by the time Edward called a halt, only because I was on the point of actually endangering Lord Anton's life without realising it. Battle fever had all but taken over, to the degree that I hardly heard the roar of the spectators and Edward's shouts to end it. I don't think Lord Anton did either; we fought on for a few moments before stopping. Then we removed our helmets and exchanged grins. We knew we had put on a very good show and had done well.

We turned back to Edward, battle-axes resting on our necks, a sign that neither of us had relinquished our weapons during the fight. Edward told us to shake hands and show our appreciation for one another as brothers in arms. I was happy to do that, whilst anxiously awaiting Edward's judgement on the days. Who would he give the honour to? We had been evenly matched during that second day.

To my relief – and surprise – the honour of both days was given to me. It was with great pride I turned to the spectators, receiving their applause and acclamation. I saw my wife standing up, applauding madly and I sent her a smile. She had been fearful of this day, worried about my being injured and I knew it.

I desperately needed to sit down as the energy was draining out through my feet and into the ground.

I desperately needed some wine, my throat felt parched and raw.

I desperately needed my wife's arms around me to assure me that all was well.

I got all three within a very short time, once I got back to my pavilion, for Elizabeth had quit the Ladies Gallery and came to attend to me. It was she who told me it had been a magnificent fight and I could relax, knowing that I had completed the emprise just as I should, in true Wydeville/Scales style. Honourably. I had to go and speak with my sister about the emprise, to see if she was happy with the way it had finally worked out, but that was a formality. If my wife was content, then so was I.

Chapter 9 - Honours

It's quite wonderful, isn't it, how one expensive emprise (at which I triumphed, of course) could lead to even higher honours. I thought I had most of it... but being given the Lordship of the Isle of Wight capped it. I had not visited the place, but was told it was beautiful, sleepy (for which I substituted undeveloped, not properly civilised, no sense of fashion and style) and had a castle. That last bit piqued my interest for I did so love castles.

As soon as practicable, Elizabeth and I packed up a few things, no, lies, lies, we arranged for some things to be packed up and we left for the south coast and the Isle of Wight.

It was enchanting. (It still is but it's got busier and full of annoying notices and tourist type things.) The castle was solidly built, was full of very good servants who rushed hither and thither and made us more than welcome and comfortable, the local dignitaries, from Oglanders onwards, invited us to visit and dine with them and all in all, I fell in love with the place. It was as simple as that.

The first visit was an amazing experience. We crossed the Solent on a calm quiet day and I thought sailing had never seemed so good. We made our way to the castle through beautiful countryside, saw some beautiful houses and wondered if we would be invited to them (we were) and watched the residents, if I may call them that, doff their caps as we went past even though they could not have known who we were. I teased Elizabeth that it was her beauty they acknowledged, she in turn told me I had Lord of the Island so firmly emblazoned on my doublet that all could read it clearly. We decided then that we were both being respectfully acknowledged and

101

that increased our good feeling at being there. Of course the truth is we were aristocracy and the peasantry acknowledged that, nothing more, nothing less but what is life if there is not fun to be found in the smallest thing?

Our escort took us to the great gates of Carisbrooke Castle and I sat and stared at it in amazement. I thought; castle on island equalled small. It didn't. It was magnificent, perfectly placed on a hill and looked out across the most peaceful landscape imaginable. And yet it had been built for protection. It was almost a contradiction in terms. I fell in love with the castle as much as I fell in love with the island.

I didn't know fully what was in Edward's mind when he gave me the Lordship of the Island, unless it was part of his devious way of giving me honours and keeping me away from court, but I know this: I treasured that beyond any other honour he awarded me. If he thought he did me a disfavour, he was wrong.

We visited the island many times over the course of the sixteen years I held the Lordship and I for one never grew tired of the place. I began some building work, planning to increase the great gateway towers. I knew they would look impressive when they were eventually done and I also instigated some essential work, such as more stables together with quarters for guests. I loved to build. There is a tremendous satisfaction in watching something grow, something you have commissioned, planned, worked on and overseen from foundations to roof.

It was about this time my father was made High Constable of England. The Wydevilles were certainly being honoured and by this time we cared nothing for what people thought of us. I recall Mother being quietly determined that it would remain that way, i.e.: high honours for the family and us not caring what people said or thought of us. If we had, none of us would have slept securely at night, that's for sure.

Life began to get busy in 1468. Well, sort of. I was appointed Lord of the Seas, pretty much a courtesy title, really, but it involved remuneration and a few committee type meetings. Nothing arduous, you understand. The key word there is remuneration. I needed to rebuild the finances after the emprise. There was money coming in from the estates but I was busy spending it and so was my wife, I have to say. She decided we needed new tapestries, new this, new that, you know how women are. Being soft as melted candle-wax where she was concerned, I said 'go ahead, dear one' not realising that would almost bankrupt me. In your terms today, I suppose you could say I was down to my last couple of million. Not enough to keep the proverbial wolf from the door, so I set about acquiring some more. Sold this piece of land and that farm, rented out this home and so on. It all helped. It kept my business manager busy, which is something. He cost me money so he had to earn his keep. Come to think of it, everything except breathing cost me money. Even that stopped in the end when I ran out of money and luck. As in, no amount of money could buy my way out of the predicament and incarceration Richard of Gloucester put me into. The bad luck for me was his misinterpretation of what was actually happening. Ah, he may well argue - I have seen this argument proposed by Ricardians everywhere - that he was right. Well, when we get to that bit we shall see, won't we, whether Ricardians are right or Woodvillians are right. I'm pleased to say there's a few more of them now than there used to be. Woodvillians, that is.

In June of that year we had the big set-piece ceremony of Margaret, the king's sister, going off to marry Charles the Bold, duke of Burgundy. Now that was something else, I can tell you. What a ceremony!

Processions and tableaux, ritual like you would not believe, just to hand over one king's sister to a duke who was as royal and as high ranking as the king. The times we lived in then dictated that we had to go about it with all due reverence. I got the task of handing her over. I also got to take my wife with me, so she was able to see and hear and remember it all. You know how women are over ceremonials like this... not that I didn't enjoy being (almost) the centre of attention... heaven forefend I should do that! Margaret was a beautiful lady in her manner and her face and her bearing. She made a good, worthy marriage, Charles the Bold was a good match for her.

After that things were relatively quiet, if you ignored the bubbling problems going on beneath the surface of court life. That was easy enough to do, if you were determined to have a good time. I was determined to have a good time but I was also wise enough not to ignore those problems, which I knew would have long lasting reverberations when they exploded. As I knew full well they would. It was just a matter of when the final blow would come and the explosion happen.

Chapter 10 - Battle lines

It got to be 1469, a turbulent year for all of us.

The simple problem was – if anything to do with Warwick could be said to be simple – Warwick himself. Denied the chance of arranging a dynastic marriage which would both favour his family and keep the king as a puppet in his hands to reinforce his chosen title of Kingmaker, he had little choice but to take up arms, if his reputation was to be upheld. Rumours ran rife around court, he was planning this, he was planning that, he had Clarence in his control and in his life, Clarence being extremely put out – and that's stating the case mildly, I have to say - that his brother the king would not allow him to marry Warwick's daughter. The tangled web went on... Edward saying he wanted Clarence to make a dynastic marriage... we laughed at that, every last one of us laughed at the nerve of the king to make such a statement when he went and did what he wanted. No more, no less. Just because he was king. Edward made a big mistake in denying Clarence his wish and I think he knew it but having said no, he could not be seen to rescind the decision. Kings didn't go back on their word, did they?

I quite liked Clarence even if he did come over sometimes as someone with an attitude, a 'look at me, I'm a York, an important one at that, take notice of me' stance. I'm not sure he would have been a brilliant king, but then, few were... that doesn't seem to matter too much in the great scheme of history. I could see how Clarence would be upset over not being able to marry the woman of his choice. I could see how he would be drawn to his strong, powerful cousin who no doubt whispered sweet nothings in his ear, words such as 'crown' 'king' 'Isabel'... and how a discontented brother might listen to said sweet nothings and agree to change sides.

I have to say though that going against your king is the height of – shall I say it outright? Stupidity. It's treason. It's high treason at that. People have been executed for less, but still... I can understand it. Even if the king happens to be your brother and by going against him you're breaking the family ties as well as the filial ties of knighthood, I can understand it. Powerful influences were at work. The lure of the crown, the promise of the bride you want, the assurance of the backing of one of the richest and most influential knights in the country... what more could any impressionable and peeved person want?

It could have put me in a predicament when the time came. I was bound by marriage to the king and had to support his cause. I was bound by friendship ties to Clarence and had to put them to one side when going out to fight. But we are not there yet, not quite, anyway.

Warwick, Clarence and an entourage, including the beautiful Isabel, set sail for Calais whilst Edward was gone. There, Clarence and Isabel were married, strictly against the king's wishes and decision. First step toward major rebellion, first step toward serious armed conflict. Invitations had gone out, London knew about the marriage and many people actually went. I mean, come on, you don't turn down a chance...

You have to understand that Warwick was one powerful man. He owned half of England, I do believe. He employed thousands of people. Thousands more lived off his power, in a manner of speaking. He had the role of a king in many ways. So, this pretender, if you like, is preparing to rebel against the king. You get an invitation to go to his daughter's wedding. What do you do, sit at home and chew your fingernails and worry if Edward will realise you did not sail to Calais for the festivities or do you hedge your bets and go, taking an expensive gift with you in your luggage, just to make sure Warwick knows you're with him? Of course they went. I couldn't. It was more than my life (wealth) was worth to do such a thing. I wished him well, silently, hoped the marriage would work, that he would be as happy as I was.

When they returned, they openly vowed their opposition to the king and their decision to try and take power for themselves. Talk about throwing down the gauntlet…

Warwick and Clarence issued proclamations blaming us Wydevilles for much of what had gone wrong. I knew about it in advance, Clarence warned me that was what Warwick had in mind and he could not dissuade him, not without giving away our secret correspondence. I told him outright it didn't matter, there was very little extra that could be added to the infamy attached to our name. What did another slander matter?

A series of uprisings had been going on here and there; some were put down, some got more serious, some demanded the king leave the arms and the bed of his wife and latest woman and get on a horse and remember that he was a soldier once. (I looked at that and thought, it's a bit harsh; perhaps I should modify it. Then I looked at it again and thought, no, that's how it was. 'Indolent' is the word that springs to mind when I think of him at that time.) Trouble is; he didn't. Instead of sorting out the rebellions, Edward decided to go on a pilgrimage of the shrines of England. I'm not sure why, maybe a little public exposure showing piety and devotion was advised. It wasn't just the uprisings, just a few people disenchanted with his rule, a few die-hard Lancastrians causing ripples, although it goes like that. First there is the wedding, then the honeymoon; then the dissension sets in. Happens with every monarch. It is one of the reasons I tended to keep my head down and stay below the parapet, let someone else stand up and take the shots. For Edward it was more than that. One report said he was 'ignorant' of the unrest going on but I doubt that very much. Edward might have been a drinking, womanising, pleasure-seeking monarch but he was astute and very little got past him. I believe, without knowing for sure, that he thought if he acted as if nothing was happening, nothing would happen. Like attracting like. It usually works, but not in this instance. I don't blame him for trying it, though; I would have done the same thing were I wearing the crown.

So he was in Norfolk in June. As the Scales family was Norfolk based, most of my property was there. We, Father, my brother John and I were accompanying the king on his pilgrimage. It was a pleasant prospect, passing the summer months trailing around the countryside as part of Edward's entourage. There were worse ways of spending my time, I thought. There was no love lost between John and myself but I adored my father. To me he was the epitome of a knight and I aspired to be as good as him in every respect. It was good to be part of a group which included him.

We were wined and dined, particularly by the Pastons, a deceitful lot. I had already tried to get Caister from them, believing it to be mine. We had a 'history'… but Sir John and I had jousted together and I admired his horsemanship. I helped with a family matter. There was talk of one of theirs marrying one of ours… but that didn't make me like them any the more. I didn't trust them or their associates. It was very much eating with your back to the wall for fear of an assassin's blade, almost. Do I over dramatise? Maybe, but at that time, paranoia meant safety. You took every precaution you could. If you were sensible, that was.

Messengers reached us there with news that the uprisings were getting a bit more serious. Edward ordered banners, armour, arms, you name it he ordered it and set out for the North. I stayed behind to get some backing for him.

Letters went out. Mostly they were ignored. You could not read a man's face and say 'you're Lancastrian at heart' but oh I longed for that ability.

It was hot. Hot and stormy that summer, as I recall and there were raised tensions all over the country to add to the ferment of discontent and heat. Edward ended up in Nottingham, getting messages and reports from all over the place, doing his best to work out what to do for the best. He sent Father and my brother John to Wales and sent letters to me in Norfolk demanding more men, more men!

There are papers and there are opinions. Here's where I tell you, the world, what happened that summer. My father and brother were sent to Wales to round up more men. I was in Norfolk co-ordinating the rounding up of more men. We were not out of the way for our health. Because... let's face facts here as we must. We were not popular with the people and we were not popular in court, either. I admit, if Edward had to return to London and tell his Queen that her father and two brothers had been killed, she would not be very happy, but then again, these were violent times and an uprising is an uprising, especially when headed by two well-known people such as Warwick and Clarence.

I repeat, to set the record straight, we were entailed to round up reinforcements for the king's cause.

The Queen had returned home. She left for London when Edward left for the north. In London she had greater security and it meant Norwich could be plundered for armed men to send north to aid the king.

There were too few and they went too late. Much too late. On the 26th July the two armies met at Edgecote. Some reports say 5000 men lay dead after three hours of fighting, others say 2000 men. It doesn't matter how many; it was a disaster for Edward and a victory for Warwick. It's known that most of the dead were Welsh.

And Edward was a prisoner of Warwick.

All this I learned later. I had my own problems before then... which my channel has had some difficulty in persuading me to discuss for this book. I relented eventually, because what is a life story without all of the life being included in it?

Whilst I had been away from Norfolk, lawlessness broke out, those who were in dispute with me over property just marched in and took it. Men invaded Middleton, a dangerous move; it was my favourite place at the time.

And I fell into the hands of Richard Roos, who had ignored my request for men at arms to be called to the king's cause and had been scheming and planning to have me as prisoner. I did not appreciate it very much.

Now, those Pastons who said my language was 'most foul' when captured at Sandwich and taken to Calais had absolutely no idea – and I mean that – of the language I used when Roos took me prisoner. I still to this day don't know who he thought he was and whether he was actually acting on orders from Warwick or Clarence (this I doubt) but I resented it more than I can tell you.

In hindsight it was almost a joke, but also in hindsight I can see that it was to replicate itself in the future, with more deadly consequences than this occasion. This could have been said to be humorous and would have been if it hadn't been so serious and if I had not been concerned for my father and brother, who were out trying to raise an army. If anyone disagreed with that... well, it's a perfect time to eliminate someone, isn't it? And was I not right to fear that, as it happened?

That is one tangled paragraph. Let me untangle it.

I was at dinner in one of the homes I owned, courtesy of the current tenant, bringing the person up to date with what was going on in the greater world, that one beyond the borders of Norfolk, I mean, when a load of armed men appeared around the building and Richard Roos walked in to put me under civil arrest. As he was heavily armed and I was not, it was easier if not safer to go with him. So I did. I was lodged at some scrofulous place known as the New Inne. And there I stayed for a few days.

I had no news. I had no messengers to bring me any news. I had no idea when I would be released. My wife had no idea where I was; she told me later she had messengers scouring the county for me without success. In times of conflict the courtesies of informing a wife where her husband is being held are simply ignored. I wondered how Mother was feeling, having no news of her husband and sons. It worried me a lot.

And then, as if by magic, the guards were not there. I walked out, a free man, borrowed a horse from a local stable with the promise of payment and rode to Sandringham, where my wife had taken refuge after the invasion of Middleton.

It was there the messenger arrived with the news of the battle of Edgecote, Edward's imprisonment by Warwick and the executions of my father and brother, who had been captured outside Coventry.

Nothing could have prepared my mind for the shock this gave me. I expected casualties, I expected a report that family members had died bravely in battle, after all they had been in several, but a cold-blooded execution when not engaged in armed conflict was appalling to me. I was ill for several weeks with total lethargy and a pain so bad I felt it to be physical and I asked my physician for something to alleviate it. The problem was, I could not cry. All the agony I felt was locked inside me and, incapable of escaping, caused the pain I was going through.

I did find the energy to write to my Mother, knowing she was going through a worse hell than I was, but even that did not help the way I felt.

Let me quash something else here... in God's name, from where do historians get their ideas? They read something in a book, a report, a line, anything and make something of it so big that it encompasses all their thinking. Or so it seems to me, reading through the many papers which abound still and worse than that, the opinions of the historians who find these papers... This is why this book and the others that are being put out have to be written. When someone posts a note on a website saying, 'I know more about the Wydevilles than you...' (a loose interpretation of the person's words, I hasten to add) I know this book has to be written for no one, no one knows more about the Wydevilles than my channel. How could they? They do not speak with us. That person was not one of us. (I know, I checked.) Perhaps they read a few books, found a few obscure articles, did a bit of research, does that make them an authority on the Wydevilles? I think not.

An historian, discussing the activities of 1469, asked the question why I too had not been executed. How did I escape he is asking, in a roundabout way. He then went on to blame it entirely on Warwick's limited authority.

It had nothing to do with that. Had Warwick decided he wanted to eliminate me as well, he would have done so without a moment's hesitation. The reason it did not happen was that I had a strong friendship with Clarence. The duke was part of my emprise; he had the 'privilege' of carrying my helm on both days. A royal prince being a servant to a mere Earl. Did you wonder why that happened, how that happened? That was the level of the friendship we had. We were friendly enough that he did not want to see me executed for nothing more than being a Wydeville. Norfolk was far enough away, he said, not to be of any real problem to Warwick and he counselled that I should live. So I did.

Let me say that no one at court, no one in Warwick's homes, knew that Clarence and I carried on a correspondence. All letters were burned for our own safety. It would not have been wise to let people know about it, so we kept it secret. My channel knew nothing of this, then or now. She has expressed her surprise and pleasure at the knowledge. It answers so many things, she said.

I knew that Clarence would stand by me and that I would stand by him, if I could. The Lord God knows that when he was incarcerated in the Tower I tried to move heaven and earth to get him released. I wanted to visit him. I wanted to write to him. All this was forbidden. The king had spoken and the king's word was the equivalent of God's word in our lives. The Lord God knows that his execution saddened me greatly. Had I known of his problem, I would have felt relief for him, more than sorrow. His book was most revealing in that regard.

Right now I would take the opportunity to counsel historians to be more careful when considering their opinions on a topic. I would suggest they look beyond the mere written word – for a change – and remember that behind every name on a sheet of paper is a person, a living, breathing, loving, hating person. Few remember it; their opinions are coloured because of it and their final words are usually erroneous because of it.

News came that Edward had eventually walked out of his 'imprisonment', much to Clarence's and Warwick's dismay, rounded up a contingent of men and marched back to London, being welcomed everywhere he went. From failure to success in one short space of time – and I have to say, for a short space of time, too. Comparatively speaking, that is. Overall, though, at the time it looked as if all was going to go well for the Soldier King.

Later I returned to court, when the pain eased, when I accepted being the 2nd Earl Rivers and began the restoration of my property. Those who had invaded my homes were thrown out, gaoled, sorted out generally and I began to feel I was in control again. Mother had gone to pieces underneath her iron mask of 'life goes on and I will go on with it'. I knew she was hurting far more than I was. She schemed the downfall or at least revenge on Warwick and Clarence and that was bad news for both of them. In turn there were those who accused her of witchcraft, but that was just the usual sort of nonsense stirred up every so often just to blacken the name of a Wydeville. They could, so they did. I knew of her total fear of being found guilty and the horrendous consequences if they had, but I also knew that the claims had little chance of being proved in court, as they were insubstantial, to put it mildly and maliciously conceived just to cause trouble. The whole thing was thrown out but it debilitated Mother, coming so soon after her unbelievable bereavement. If there was one thing us children knew, it was that we did not exist when Father was around. She lived for him and him alone. Without him she was hard put to survive. No one could take his place.

There were problems. There were uprisings. There were headaches all round for Edward. I listened and kept my counsel at all times. He set out with a small army to put down the insurrections, apparently firing off letters in all directions as he did so and beheading a few people, too, those who went against his will. Warwick and Clarence were ordered to appear before the king at the end of March, but they fled. They tried to escape by sea but in my role as Lord of the Seas, I managed to block them. Now you see what I meant about taking sides. I had to obey the king's commands and block the escapees. They got free eventually, though, and set sail for France.

And, despite my being Lieutenant of Calais, somehow that title was handed to Hastings. Oh did ever that burn in my heart! Not because I resented the title being taken from me as much as the person it was given to. Hastings and I were mostly at daggers drawn 99% of the time. We simply hated each other. It was hate at first sight, I'm afraid. He didn't much like any Wydeville, but me... he hated me more than any of the others. That says a lot, considering how many 'others' there were. He had to be polite to my sister, he had to be polite to me but underneath the 'niceness' seethed a heart full of hatred. I was awarded my father's position of Constable of England but in a fit of pique, which I couldn't tell anyone about, I resigned, said I had too much to do. It was a lie but a convincing one.

I wasn't there so I can't say what went on Over There, but something did go on Over There, because Warwick was not a man to stand still and take whatever Edward was going to throw at him. He would have been seething over his inability to sail freely away from England and I heard tell that they were blocked from landing anywhere for a month. Later I heard that Clarence's son had been born on board ship because of the refusal to allow them to land – and the child died. Warwick would have been incensed with that, a grandchild sacrificed to politics, a power struggle between the king and his cousin had resulted in the death of an innocent.

Talk flashed around court: Warwick was raising an army, Clarence was contrite and wanted to come back, Warwick wanted peace, Clarence wanted war – in the end no one knew what to believe. No one would say or could say where the rumours were coming from, what they were based on, reports that were half heard, no reports at all... no one knew. It was safer to dismiss it all until the truth was heard from the mouths of those who were there. Nothing else would do. I found out about the child later, when Clarence wrote secretly to me. I knew before anyone else and told no one, apart from my beloved Elizabeth who could keep a secret as well as I.

The one thing that was certain, more certain than even the fact that Edward had seriously miscalculated Warwick's intentions, in my opinion anyway, was that he, Warwick, was Up To Something over there and that Something did not bode well for Edward.

We found out what that Something was when the invasion army, as it were, arrived in England and declared for Henry VI. That put a considerable number of cats among a vast flock of pigeons, I can tell you! People scampered and dashed and rushed hither and thither. Edward marshalled his army and once again we set out to do battle.

We, as in Gloucester, Hastings, Howard, Say and the king, were in Doncaster when a messenger arrived – interrupting our meal, as it happens – with the news that Montagu, supposedly bringing an army to Edward's cause, had decided to swap allegiance. At that point Edward decided flight was the only thing left and we were all detailed to go with him. It seemed a fraction of time between eating and leaving. We were riding wildly for the coast with a retinue of armed men. I don't know how many, as truthfully, it never occurred to me to count them, but just as with the torches at Calais... historians have made up their own minds. So, pick a number anywhere between one hundred and eight hundred and somewhere in there is the right answer, such is the variety of estimates in the variety of books on the Wars of the Roses. My question is; how did anyone come up with a number anyway? No one counted them, as far as I know. Let's consider this: Edward's intention was to flee to the Continent. In all seriousness, would you take eight hundred men with you, to be fed, watered and sheltered by someone over there? Would that not be stretching hospitality just a little too far? We had no money, no possessions, nothing. We were on the march; we were ready for battle, not an extended holiday across the Channel. In truth, even five hundred men would be too many. My educated guess is that we had about four – five hundred to escort us to the coast and about a hundred all told who went with us. That was enough to guard the king and his four companions. Any more would look like an army being routed, any less would leave us open to a charge of insufficient security for the king.

It was cold, as I remember. It was worrying, that was a fact. We rode flat out, full gallop for the coast, Edward shouting instructions to us and the men accompanying us. Gloucester, true to form, said nothing. Hastings hardly stopped talking until Edward told him to save his breath. Say was quiet, keeping things to himself, only agreeing with his king occasionally. I don't think I spoke much; I was busy wondering how long it would be before I could hold my wife again. No, make that worrying about how long it would be before I could hold my wife again. This was exile, not a pleasure trip. This was flight, whether we wanted to call it that or a strategic retreat. I didn't want to be there but I was there. As we rode, surrounded by armed men, I contemplated the fact that sometimes having dinner was a dangerous occupation. I had been taken prisoner in Norwich after eating and here I was, fleeing for the coast, because I had dinner with Edward, Gloucester and the others.

Foolishly, I forgot this in 1483... but more of that later.

Kings Lynn was silent, dark, with a cold wind coming off the sea and very few ships at anchor. Three, actually. We commissioned them on behalf of the King, paying for the passage with all the gold we had between us and Edward's fur-lined cloak. I thought, he'll regret that later, but needs must – we had to get out of England. Edward detailed men to be his armed guard for the journey and dismissed the rest. I took over then, sent them off to my various homes with messages to those in charge to take them in, feed, shelter and care for them, store the arms and then, when it got a bit quieter, let them return to their homes with pay for their time in service. And to keep a note of what they paid out so I could recoup it later from the Treasury. It solved the problem of the men and told everyone, including my beloved wife, what was happening. I managed to enclose a personal letter for her, hastily written, along with the instructions for some of the however many hundred men she had to accommodate at Sandringham.

We were on board and under sail within an hour. Destination, the home of Duke Charles of Burgundy. We had to hope he would welcome us. Edward said he would. Hastings said he had no choice if we turned up on his doorstep. Gloucester said nothing but the glowering looks he gave everyone said everything. Not my favourite person but he didn't rank as high in the 'not my favourite person' list as Hastings. It was going to be tough, this exile. No wife, no homes, no money, but hey, look, I had Hastings for company. Sometimes loyalty to your king is stretched a little thin…

Before us, an unknown time in exile. Behind us, England in confusion, a pregnant Queen, a headless government, rebels everywhere and a – should I say this? a monkish ineffectual king about to take over again, pushed by his scheming avaricious wife. I didn't know this for sure at the time but some things are as certain as taxes. The king had fled = confusion.

Pregnant Queen: Elizabeth was constantly pregnant. Rebels everywhere = reason we were fleeing. Reason for rebels: Henry VI was about to be reinstated as king and the Lancastrians were once again taking over. Warwick did not dare do anything else. He could not assume the throne himself, Clarence was not able to take over – there were two living kings at that time, let's not compound the problem by making it three – and only Margaret of Anjou could contrive such a coup. It all made perfect sense to me. Headless government; they had no idea what to do, who to serve, who was the strongest person to tell them what to do.

Later, all this was confirmed in despatches to Edward. I hadn't been wrong anywhere in my conclusions. I kept my own spy network busy and had a pretty good idea of what was happening and where it was happening most of the time. I confess, though, that the Montagu defection came as a surprise. Racing to exile did not. Somehow I anticipated that would happen. I just wished I had someone to pack a bundle of clothes for me. I do so hate wearing the same doublet two days in succession.

It was raining when we arrived.

Well, if I'm honest, it rained from the moment we left Kings Lynn; it rained all across the Channel so that, combined with the spray, made it a very unpleasant journey. There's one thing I hate more than wearing the same doublet two days in succession; wearing a wet one. My cloak was gallantly handed over to my king, you see…

So we arrived, wet, weary and broke, knocked on the front door and said to the minion who opened it, eventually, "Edward IV, King of England, Gloucester, Say, Hastings and Rivers, along with an assorted bunch of armed men, crave shelter for the next X amount of days/weeks/months till he can get his crown back."

He took one look at the bedraggled bunch (I am shorter than Edward so my cloak didn't quite fit – as I said, I'd handed it over to him) and shut the door in our faces.

So we looked at one another and knocked again. It seems he had gone off to get someone with some sense as this time when the door opened we were allowed in.

All right, maybe it wasn't quite like that ... but near enough. We were one very wet bedraggled group by the time we reached His Grace's home as it had rained consistently and persistently throughout the journey. No one was speaking at all by the time we arrived, saddle sore, starving, exhausted and angry. Edward has a Look when he gets angry, he'd been wearing it from the moment he heard of Montagu's defection and the rain just made it worse. Edward Not Speaking is often worse than Edward Speaking, because when he's ranting and raving you get some idea of what's going on in his head. Silence is scary. Then you have no idea what's going on in his head but you can be sure it isn't pleasant.

What can I say about exile other than it was tedious, distressing (for me anyway, being away from all I loved) worrying (we only had vague rumours of what was going on in England) confining (it was Not Nice weather and we couldn't get away from one another very much) and altogether was not the way I expected – or wanted - to spend my time. I was more than glad when Edward began seriously talking about ships and getting back to England as soon as possible once the Christmas festivities, such as they were, finally ended. Oh, we had as good a time as you can in someone else's house with someone else's kitchens and cellar for wine and ale and a limited supply of money to buy gifts. We all promised one another that next Christmas would be better, we'd be back in England with our wealth restored, so we could make up for the fact this Christmas we didn't give much at all, apart from our word to make it better next time.

We all had something to do when the plans were formulated, instead of playing endless games of Tables, drinking too much and destroying the reputations of both Clarence and Warwick in the privacy of the rooms we were given. We had to be a little bit careful, people tended to eavesdrop all the time and sell their information on. Didn't I know it well; I ran my spy network on just that premise. Warwick was likely to have informants just about everywhere, behind every door and in every stable, hovering at every meal and stalking us through every walk or ride we took. All right, perhaps paranoia was taking over a bit – just a bit, you understand – but being away from home because you had to be away from home not because you wanted to be did strange things to your mind. Mine, anyway. I wondered whether Edward was missing his Queen very much. I knew he found solace in quite a few soft welcoming arms but they were not Elizabeth's arms and for all his talk, I knew he cared for my sister. It was the one thing I liked very much about him. I knew how much I was missing my Elizabeth and I didn't seek solace in any soft and welcoming arms, because it wouldn't have been right. I couldn't have lived with my conscience if I had. Not that there weren't invitations, there were, lots of them but they bypassed me and they bypassed Gloucester, too. He wore his 'dark' look which worried me more than Edward's Not Speaking and angry look. With Gloucester you could never guess what he was thinking – or scheming. Up front he was loyal and devoted to his brother, sharp to the point of rudeness with us if we dared question how he felt, what he thought, what he planned to do when we returned to England – we always said when, not if, no exile lasts forever unless the person dies and none of us planned on doing that – so we left him alone. But playing Tables with someone who wore their 'dark' look all the time was not much fun. I left Edward and Hastings to do that and took refuge in my room where I penned endless letters to my wife and bribed people to get them sent to England. I know over half of them arrived, which is a miracle in itself. None of Elizabeth's got through to me, although she sent some, then gave up when my letters made it clear they weren't arriving. Oh my poor wife, alone and worried, with all the estates to run and decisions to make and winter coughs and chills to cope with. I longed ceaselessly for the exile to end so I could just go home and be with her. I doubt I was a good companion for anyone at that time.

Then the preparations began for the return to England. Bad weather held us up for some time and if I tell you that when we actually did set sail, we ran into a storm so ferocious that we lost a ship with men and horses, it'll give you some idea of how bad the weather was that prevented us from setting sail in the first place. The ships lost touch with each other and we all landed on different parts of the coast. The most important thing was that Edward, Gloucester, Hastings, Say and myself, of course, all survived the crossing although I knew well we were all extremely pleased to set foot on dry land again. With a little negotiation here and there we all met up, looked at each other's bedraggled condition and decided we had to do something about it before we began the march to London, our ultimate destination. We were on the Yorkshire coast so we headed for York. We collected a few men along the way, those who were well pleased to see us and we made our way to the great city on the pretext of supporting King Henry. It was a smart move, the gates swung open to let us in, we were welcomed; given dry clothes, food, ale and, best of all, a bed that didn't sway or resonate with the sound of a howling gale and waves smashing against the wood. For a long time, each night I went to my bed that was all I heard.

And so, with acquired horses, with some money from the people of York to buy provisions along the way, we began the long trek to London. Edward was extremely keen to get there, knowing that by the time he arrived he would have a new child to fuss over. I just wanted to get to London so I could quickly visit my business manager, assure myself that all was well and head for Sandringham. Whatever the politics of the day, whatever was going on in London, I needed to be with my wife.

There has been much discussion over the years as to what happened to Henry VI when Edward arrived in London. My information is that he was taken to the Tower and there given the royal rooms. And there he died. I'm not going to speculate on what happened. The historians have been playing with this for a very long time, trying to blame it on Gloucester or just about anyone else who happened to be in the Tower at that time. They are determined that he was murdered, but I have to say the frailty of the man has to be taken into consideration. The shock of suddenly being deposed, taken away from his palace, put back in the Tower, his wife racing into exile, could well have been enough for his overtaxed heart. It is much more convenient to blame a murder on someone who later attracted a whole string of murders to his name without him doing a single thing to justify it, that is if you except Hastings' peremptory execution and that of myself, my nephew and Thomas Vaughan. But that came about through a series of misunderstandings which at that time he took to be fact. But we are a long way from that and I'll go into that in greater detail when the time comes. What I'm saying now is; you cannot in hindsight blame someone for the death of someone else without proof. Yes it was inconvenient to have two Kings; yes it was inconvenient that one had to be in one place and one in another. It did not necessarily mean that you had to send in an assassin. Maybe Edward did order an execution, but in truth I don't think so. If I'm wrong, I am sure he'd tell me. What I'm saying to you is, grant him the benefit of the doubt.

I needs must tell you that when we got to Westminster Abbey, I saw Edward with his firstborn son in his arms. Edward, Prince of Wales, had arrived whilst we were on the continent. He was a fine child. I greeted my sister the Queen, visited my mother who was too busy to speak with me, being in charge of everything that went on relating to my sister's stay at the Abbey – why did I get the distinct impression the staff would be well pleased to see the back of them all? – realised that Elizabeth was tired, happy, relieved that her husband was back in England and was making arrangements to leave the Abbey, which set me free. I, in turn, was busy making arrangements to leave London and get to Norfolk as fast as a horse could carry me. I had an Elizabeth waiting for me, too.

Chapter 11 - Battles

I was not able to stay long to enjoy my wife's caresses, to walk around our favourite home, to see what had gone on during my absence. I knew I shouldn't have gone, I knew there were problems looming, but I had to see her for myself and hold her in my arms to assure her that I was really back in England and that all was well. The estates were a poor second, but reason enough to go. Conflict called again, the array had gone out so I returned to London to find we were going into battle against Warwick. So the armour came out of its mothballs once again, the men at arms I had on the payroll once again faced marching into danger with me. The strange thing is, even though I held Warwick responsible for the death of my father and my brother, I had little stomach for the fight this time. My thoughts were that perhaps I had been out of England too long, that my taste for battle had been cooled by the exile, or quite simply that I hadn't been home long enough with my wife for me to feel at ease in leaving her again so soon. I dared not tell anyone such a thing, it's important to times to show a courageous face, especially when you're part of the army your King is leading into battle. He would scorn any signs of what he would call cowardice. It wasn't fear which held me back, I had no fear of the fight so what was the problem? Elizabeth put her finger on it by chance one night, the night before I left, in truth.

"You have learned to see both sides, my beloved husband. You can no longer see black and white which lets you charge into battle with full knowledge of 'right' being on your side.' It was true. My friendship with Clarence had made me aware of the other side of the argument. Whilst my loyalty had to remain with my king, as his brother-in-law I had little chance of doing anything else. I wasn't as committed to this battle as I might have been. The consequences of this were that I was wounded for the first time.

And so we marched to Barnet where Warwick had his forces waiting for us. Edward deployed his men and, before I knew what was happening, battle was engaged. My brother Edward was fighting with us. I saw him account for several men and I knew that I'd slain a few as well before someone got lucky and I took a sword thrust in my side. I fought on for a while but then had to retire from the battlefield for I was losing blood fast and it was weakening me. The surgeon cleaned the wound as best he could and sewed it together, then bound it tight. I waited out the battle, wanting to know that my men were all right, before giving the orders to return home. And so it was I knew that Warwick had been struck down on the battlefield. When we returned to London, I went to see my mother to let her know that I was alive but wounded, knowing how she worried about each of us and then was able to tell her that Warwick was dead and that unfortunately a Woodville had not been responsible for this. I know that Mother would have been much happier if that had been the case.

Mother's appearance shocked me. I had seen her for such a short time when we arrived at the Abbey, where she was shrouded in thick furs and robes against the cold. Then she was busy and bustling, issuing orders in every direction, ensuring that the new-born child was taken care of and that my sister was not only having the rest she needed but continued to have the respect accorded to a Queen. I hadn't realised just how much of a toll Father's death had taken on her. There, in the quietness of her rooms, I could look at her properly. She looked old and frail. I had no doubt she was in sorrow and grief for John as well, but the truth was it was Father's death which caused the change in her. I tried not to show it; as much as she was trying hard not to show me how shocked she was that I was tired, possibly thinner and obviously in pain. I couldn't hide the fact that the wound was quite bad.

I stayed the night so we could talk and then went home to my wife. It was a long and arduous journey, but I would have travelled halfway around the world to get back to her. Whatever was wrong with me, her ministrations would cure it.

I wasn't able to fight at the Battle of Tewkesbury, because the wound had not healed and I had little strength in my arm. I heard of the great victory Edward managed to achieve, but I also heard of the violation of sanctuary and admitted to myself and to my Elizabeth I was glad I wasn't there. I couldn't have tolerated something so dreadful. I would have had to say something and that wouldn't have gone down very well with the King.

With Warwick buried, Clarence back in the Yorkist fold, the Prince of Wales dead on the battlefield and Anne Neville free to marry, which meant Gloucester could finally achieve his aim, I hoped that life would begin to settle down. Margaret of Anjou was no longer a force to be reckoned with, without her husband and son she had little to bargain with and so I could see that there was little that could disrupt Edward's rule. Was it possible that the endless clashes, battles, arguments, were finally over?

A benevolent Edward, keen to show his new stature as he began his second period as king, appointed me ambassador to the Duke of Bretagne, Governor to the young Prince of Wales and made me Chief Butler of England. All of this was extremely influential and I welcomed the honours. It almost compensated for the time in exile, although anything which took me away from my wife was not to be considered as worth having.

If the period of my life when I was married to Elizabeth, daughter of Thomas Scales, reads like a romance, then so be it. I can only tell you the truth. She was the light of my life and, as you will find out later, her passing took that light out of my life and it was quite a few years before I found someone who could even begin to replace her. Forgive me if this is not a manly attitude to take, it is nothing more or less than the truth.

By including intensely personal information such as this, I hope to contribute to the ongoing series of books which aims to bring life to people who have been, up to now, nothing but a name in history. It is easy for historians to say for example, Richard Wydeville and John Wydeville were executed after the battle of Edgecote. They are right to do this if it is an academic work, but it would help the casual reader if the historians were to acknowledge that the executions of my father and brother caused utter devastation to my mother and my sisters and brothers, not to mention myself. It may be trite to quote John Donne here but I will:

No man is an island entire of himself. Ask not for whom the bell tolls, it tolls for thee.

Each death on the battlefield, each execution following a battle leaves behind heartache for some, hardship for others, if not a combination of the two. Each death brings its own grief, so while we discuss coldly the fact that Warwick was struck down on the battlefield at Barnet, we must remember that he had family, loyal retainers and servants, together with a vast amount of employees, some of whom thought very highly of him. There is also the unspoken grief of the Yorks; they had lost a cousin who had been extremely influential in their lives. Where then in history books is there any mention of regret for the death of the Earl? It isn't there, for it's not something that people do.

For the same reason, you won't find records anywhere that my marriage was very happy and that I was anything other than totally devastated when she died. Believe it or not, history is actually made up of people, not of cyphers. Although it may seem at times as if we're no more than the pawns on a chessboard, we are in fact human and as such carry all the emotions you do. It would be good if more people realised this and, instead of having to write fiction to create each person as a living human being, it could be shown in the more serious books of history. Alas, I don't see this happening.

That lecture having been concluded, I needs must return to my life story. I had a good life for a while, even as I watched my mother declining, for I was busy with the many duties my new honours brought with them. I wanted a short time away and thought I would go to Portugal, having in my mind a need to go on a pilgrimage, but eventually I decided not to. I had been given permission to leave court and so I took the opportunity to go to Lindisfarne instead.

The word 'pilgrimage' has not been mentioned in this account so far and so I need to explain why I felt the need to do this.

It had a great deal to do with the fact I was seriously wounded. The wound itself was not lethal; it was the infection which I generated in it subsequently which caused many problems. It was during my convalescence that I had time to think on what might have been, rather than what was. It could easily have been my last battle; had any major organs been pierced, I would have not survived. I already had a high degree of piety, but following this illness, for that is what it was, I found myself needing to spend more time thinking and praying to my God. Elizabeth encouraged me in this when she realised how important it was to my recovery and it was she who suggested a journey to Lindisfarne rather than to Portugal. For one thing it cut out a lengthy sea journey, for another the people would speak English. For my first venture into a time of quiet withdrawal, Elizabeth thought I would be better with those who spoke English, as they would be able to offer spiritual comfort and prayers if I needed it.

I saw the logic of her argument and went north to Lindisfarne.

To say that the conditions there were basic about sums them up. I was used to luxury, soft beds, soft covers, plentiful food and constant companionship. At Lindisfarne I found myself fighting a different kind of battle. I learned to eat plain food, to drink pure water, to spend much time in silence and to sleep on a hard bed with just one coverlet. I didn't find it comfortable, but it was challenging and I was able to use the times of silence to consider my way of life. I spent many hours in prayer and an equal amount of time waiting for God's answer. The one thing I did learn during my time there was that if you ask, you must wait for an answer. I said there was silence, but in truth Lindisfarne isn't silent. The wind is constant, the waves are constant; the seabirds are constant. It takes time to stop listening to them and to listen to that which is within. I knew after my first visit there that I wouldn't achieve what I set out to achieve in such a short time. In fact I returned to Lindisfarne on several occasions and each time was able to go deeper into the silence and to benefit from it. I found the experience humbling, which was good for me. I was happy to display my wealth, the other side of me, in London, in Grafton and at my homes in Norfolk and Hertfordshire, for that's the way people expected me to be. Only when I went on pilgrimages could the quieter, more introspective side of me reveal itself. The only other person who ever saw this was my wife. She had her own very deep faith which sustained her through our absences, especially during my time in exile, when she said that was all that had kept her going.

She understood the need for silence and we would often walk or sit in the gardens of our homes not speaking, sometimes not even touching; doing nothing more than listening to God's world. In that, we found a deeper relationship than we ever thought possible. A coming together of two souls is something which happens on several levels. There is the first immediate level of attraction, the person must in some way be agreeable in the eyes of the other. The second is the emotion which this attraction generates, which some call love, but which I believe comes later, when the attraction and the lust settles, turning itself into the deeper emotion which is known as love. From then on the emotions can, in the perfect relationship, go on to a higher level, a joining together of two souls. Not everyone finds their soul mate in their lifetime. I wonder sometimes if my mother had not befriended Lady Scales whether Elizabeth and I would have met. I like to think that Fate, the Angels, whatever you want to call it, would have found a way to bring us together if our respective mothers hadn't done so. I am grateful I had eleven wonderful years with my wife. Had I had my way, those eleven years would have been thirty or forty or even fifty years.

It was not to be.

At the end of May, Mother died. She was a broken woman at the end. Her own battles, to keep us all in good favour in court, to have a daughter anointed Queen of England, to fight to live with her own grief at Father's death and her son John who meant so much to her, the battle to disprove the stupid vindictive witchcraft allegations, all took their toll on someone who had given her all to life. We buried her in Grafton, her favourite place, after a lengthy procession through the surrounding area to give all who had come to rely on her a chance to pay their respects. I was astonished at the amount of people who came out to just stand by the side of the road and watch the procession go by. We counted no cost in giving her a wonderful funeral, just as she had never counted the cost of giving us all a wonderful life. Elizabeth came with a magnificent guard of honour, but inside that grandeur was a daughter mourning a mother who had been her counsellor, guide and helper throughout the difficult times, the exile, the births, everything. Mother had been there for her.

My Elizabeth stood by my side and watched as the woman she admired was lowered into the ground and commented afterwards how gentle the gravediggers were when they filled in the grave. It was as if they didn't wish to hurt Mother in any way.

And we returned to London to try and put a life together that had no central figure in it. It felt empty and strange for a very long time.

In July I was commissioned to take an armed force to Brittany to negotiate an alliance with the Duke. I asked for and gained permission to take my wife with me, as I didn't think I could bear to be separated from her again. How did I know our time together was short? It was there that our world began to fall apart.

It was September, the prelude to our favourite season, when one night I reached for my wife's breast with my left hand whilst caressing her with the right one. Her flesh was soft, malleable – and had a lump just below the surface. I went completely cold and must have recoiled from her for she knew immediately something was wrong. Her hand went to the same breast; she moved her fingers and knew what I had found.

A death sentence.

I tried to be encouraging, I told her I would get our physician to take a look, maybe it was not what we thought it was, no, it could be just fat, could be anything… we lied to one another with frozen faces. We made love in the most gentle manner imaginable, trying to console one another and convey with our bodies what our mouths could not say.

I didn't sleep that night. I heard the sounds of the house where we were staying, heard the timbers settle and creak, heard the sound of the wildlife outside our window, which was partly open to the cool early Autumn air, heard the snuffle and bang of horses shifting in the stables. I heard the beating of my heart and wondered if it would go on beating after 'the' event. I couldn't visualise living without my Elizabeth. I told myself to stop being stupid, it could be anything but everything told me what it was. I couldn't deny it.

I wanted to cry, to release the pent-up feelings, but no tears would come. So I lay there, dry-eyed and hurting, for the remainder of the dark hours, anticipating more dark hours to come. I heard Elizabeth's breathing, gentle, rhythmic, something I had loved from the moment we were married. I had not been home enough. I had spent time in London for the foolish tournament and delegated much of the estate work to her. I had spent time in Grenewich waiting for my opponent, leaving her in Westminster with my mother. I had been in exile with Edward, I had gone to Brittany on Edward's business, I had gone to Lindisfarne.

During the lonely dark hours I regretted every single night we had spent apart knowing, with a cold certainty, our time together was going to be cut short by one small lump.

I could conceal nothing from my wife. The moment she opened her eyes and looked at me, she knew I hadn't slept. She started to berate me for it and then stopped, her eyes full of tears and said, "I'm sorry I slept."

"Foolish creature," I told her. "It was my choice to stay awake!" A lie but she need not know that, I thought. I wish I had slept, I would not have had so long in which to envisage the unbelievable: life without Elizabeth.

I'm not sure who I thought I was fooling. She saw right through that and pretended to attack me. We rolled on the bed together, laughing.

"I'm not dead yet," she told me. "Let's not anticipate anything."

She was right and I knew it. But the pain would not leave me.

The physician came, inspected the lump, looked worried and told her he would like to cut it out. She agreed immediately. I was horrified at the thought of her delightful body being scarred but knew that it might save her life. So the lump was cut out and burned.

"Now you see I'll be fine," she told me, when she came round from the laudanum he had used to dope her.

She wasn't fine. It took weeks for the wound to heal, it suppurated, it pained, it had to be cleaned and she suffered terribly. But she remained cheerful and determined that nothing would defeat her. We told each other the cancer had gone. We said she had years of life ahead and much to do in that time. We said we would go to Europe, see the great sights; do the things we always said we would do when we had freedom from court and the estates. We planned our journeys, writing long sheets of possible locations. We laughed and were busy fooling ourselves. We didn't say, either of us, that she was easily tired, very pale, not the person she had been before the operation. Before The Lump, as I thought of it. I told myself it was the wound which was the cause of it and knew I was fooling no one, let alone myself.

We returned to England in November, when sickness swept through the regiment and decimated it. There was nothing I could do there and I knew Elizabeth was declining, even though she denied it. I was just grateful that I had the time with her; time that I knew was running out. Had I been in Brittany and she back in England... it didn't bear thinking about.

We went to London for the Twelve Days of Christmas, vowing to enjoy ourselves. We had gifts to distribute, my daughter to visit, my brothers and sisters to placate for we had not seen them very much, having been out of the country for so long. No one knew of her condition and Elizabeth made me promise I would say nothing.

"My problem," she said earnestly, before we left. "My problem and my need for privacy. I don't want false sympathy and gushing sentimentality."

So we went with brave faces and aching hearts, for Elizabeth tired too quickly for my liking, even faster than before. She could not stay at the dances very long; we had to find excuses to put to Edward so that we could leave without offending him. Fortunately for us, court was crowded and he was not overly concerned whether we were there or not. As soon as the festivities were finished, we went home, pleading pressure of estate business, but really to get her back to the place she loved most of all where she didn't have to act as if all was well. We knew it wasn't, we knew she was very ill but neither of us spoke of it. We continued with our plans to go to Europe, to see Florence and Rome and Venice and -

By the sacred festival of Easter in 1473, Elizabeth was visibly losing weight and was very much worse. Clothes hung on her as if made for someone three times her size. She tired so quickly; she could manage only the shortest journey on horseback. She ate virtually nothing and vomited up any wine she drank, even watered down. Her mind began wandering; her decisions about the household made little or no sense. I relied heavily on our housekeeper, Mistress McAllister, a wonderful motherly person who watched the

135

deterioration in my wife and quietly assumed control of the house, the grounds and servants without being asked. It was done almost without our noticing it. Anything Elizabeth said or ordered was noted. If it was sensible, it was carried out, if it wasn't, it was quietly ignored and she didn't notice. The house and everything around it ran smoothly, there were no arguments, no problems which needed my attention. Food was bought or grown and prepared, meals were cooked, animals were tended, the house was clean and tidy and nothing was said about the Mistress's lack of direction. Everyone knew what was happening; no one wanted to say the word. It was a shadow in every room, behind every person, even stalking the grounds.

I was afraid of hurting the skeletal figure which occupied so little of our marital bed, afraid of rolling on her and breaking something in the night, she was that fragile. In June I arranged for one of the other bedrooms to be prepared for her. It was a sunny, pleasant room with windows overlooking the countryside. Fresh breezes would be able to come in to lift the sick room air and leave it cleansed. We were going through another long hot summer and I wanted her to be as cool as it was possible for her to be.

In a moment of what I think of as a peculiarity, I ordered that everything which related to her condition, potions, bowls, towels, whatever, were to be put in a cabinet out of sight, so that no one entering the room would know it was occupied by an invalid. I hated the thought of her being surrounded by items that screamed 'sickness' to the world. I brought in a couple of her favourite tapestries, silver candlesticks I knew she liked, a bowl that was beautiful by its very existence, anything to make the room something she would appreciate. And finally I ordered fresh flowers to be put by her bed every day.

She said nothing when I told her of the arrangements, didn't argue with me for or against the move, but sighed with what seemed like contentment when I scooped her up and carried her to her new room. She weighed nothing at all; I could have carried her round the entire boundary of Sandringham and not wearied.

I sat her down on the bed and she looked round. "I've always favoured this room," she said with one of her sweet smiles. "Thank you, beloved husband." Then she fell back onto the pillow and closed her eyes. Even that small journey from one end of the corridor to the other had tired her.

Court was forgotten, the estates were forgotten; the horses had to be exercised by others. I sent letters to my business manager, Andrew Dymock, authorising him to deal with everything in my absence and to trouble me as little as possible. 'My wife is dying' I scrawled on the end of one letter. He would understand. He knew my devotion to Elizabeth. I wrote formally to Edward, explaining the situation and had a heartfelt letter of condolence in return, giving me leave to remain away from court as long as it took.

Mistress McAllister's husband found a large comfortable chair in one attic and brought it down for me. Except when the nurses were there and when I went to bathe, eat and eventually to sleep, I sat in the chair by her side, holding her hand, talking softly when she was awake – not very often – and just looking at her when she slept. The flesh fell from her face, exposing a bone structure that was beautiful in its own way. I knew she would have been a stately, striking old lady and sorrowed she would not live to be the person I could see being revealed. Her ladies came, more out of duty than anything, to offer their services. In the end I dismissed them, much to their relief, for there was nothing they could do and nothing I wanted them to do but leave my wife with me for the weeks left to us.

When she was awake, we would study her Book of Hours together and contemplate the paintings; we would murmur the prayers together from her prayer book. We would talk of things we had done and people we had met and marvelled at how much we had shared in our eleven years of marriage. It felt much, much longer than that.

By the end of August I knew the end was approaching and asked the priest to be on call for her. I would know when I needed to call him but when I did, I wanted an immediate response.

Elizabeth's voice had grown faint; she hardly existed as a person anymore. Her limbs were even more skeletal than before, she could not be touched without being bruised. I spent more and more time with her, rushing through bathing, only eating half the meals, aware that the weight was dropping from me as well but not caring at that time. I resented the time I spent sleeping but knew I had to sleep to stay strong enough to sit with her and watch her die.

There are many terrible things in life that human beings have to endure. Watching your beloved wife die is to me the worst of them all. Watching because you're helpless to do anything else, you can't arrest the disease and send it away; you can't stop the flesh from failing, the spirit from giving up. You're caught in a trap of your own making, the love you have for the woman who is leaving you behind.

Early in September I called the priest to administer the Last Rites. Elizabeth was fading before my eyes. I wanted her to know what was happening, not have the oil touched to a lifeless body. I could see by her eyes she was pleased and her lips moved as she whispered the words along with the priest. I could see by his eyes he was deeply moved. He put a hand on my shoulder when he was through.

"My son, your devotion is exceptional."

"Father, my wife is exceptional."

He bowed his head. "This I know. She will be a great loss to you. May God protect and strengthen you."

He left then, which was just as well; I couldn't have stood much more of his compassion. It was all I could do to be strong for Elizabeth.

She lay silent, on her back, a small smile curving the lips I loved so much. The September sun shone in the window onto her, lighting her face, sparkling in her hair. For a moment she was the woman I had met and married years ago. I sat and stared and went back in my memory, reliving all those wonderful times we shared, visiting Carisbrooke Castle, travelling to places in the north, staying in our beautiful home at Newcelles, her gentleness with my natural daughter and how she never ever reproached me or herself for the fact our marriage was childless. It didn't matter, only she was important to me.

I don't know how long it was from the time the priest left until the moment I realised the hand I was holding was stiff and chilled. It could have been minutes; it could have been the rest of the day. I don't know, I've never asked.

All I knew was that she had gone and I put my head on her withered body and sobbed.

I could fight any battle but not that one. I could face any enemy, but not that one. Sandringham became a prison. I stormed around in it, raging against fate for taking my wife from me, raging against doctors who couldn't save the most precious person in my life, all the while understanding the levels of grief which I was enduring.

The battle went on for weeks until I finally gave way to accepting my beloved had left me to live on alone. It took a lot of accepting but I got there and then began to plan the rest of my life, however long fate had for me.

Chapter 12 - New interests

My faith meant a great deal to me. Where most people paid lip service to the church, attending Mass to be seen by those of us who were taking the sacraments, for me it was real. It was my very anchor during the solitary months after the grief finally let me live a somewhat normal life again.

I regularly went to stay at Lindisfarne on silent retreats, where I could spend time going inward, thinking my way round the many problems that confronted me, which I had to face alone. I once took them to Elizabeth and we talked them through together, sometimes at dinner, sometimes walking in the gardens, sometimes by the hearth with mulled ale or wine. In the silence of the stones at Lindisfarne, with only the sound of the endless relentless sea crashing against the rocks, I could come to terms with my loss and seek my love through the quieting of my mind.

I must of necessity include my second marriage, so I will slot the information in here. Mary Fitzlewis became my second wife in 1481. She was never a substitute wife, should anyone think that way. I had genuine affection and fondness for her, she was attractive, intelligent, quiet and most of all, loyal. It was obviously a failing in me that the second marriage did not produce an heir.

So, although being married gave me anchorage in a time of great distress, the smallest thing would revive a memory of my beloved wife, I needed the distraction of travel. Pilgrimages did much to settle my agonised mind. From then it was but a short step to going on pilgrimages in Europe. This did not meet with the approval of the King, but then Edward ever was single minded and all powerful and could not understand the depth of my grief. Before I remarried, he kept throwing names at me, potential wives. He could not accept my Elizabeth was everything to me.

Europe distracted me for a while, different scenery, faces, voices and buildings, above all the beautiful buildings, but I could never stay as long as I would have liked, my role of tutor to the new Prince of Wales had to come first. As it was there were rumours, talk that I was not taking the role seriously. As always, I dismissed all this talk whilst storing it for the future, knowing what people were saying about you was half the battle to overcoming it.

The story of the book is well known, but as always there is far more behind any single act than is seen by the rest of the world. I met William Caxton on one of my pilgrimages when I was actually doing diplomatic work for Edward. He happened to be at one of the gatherings and gave me an opportunity to see his printing process for myself. I had heard talk of it and found it totally absorbing and fascinating.

It was a 'coincidence' that it was that journey to Europe which saw me come home with the book The Dictes and Sayinges of the Philosophres, which I immediately began to translate from French into English. I had in mind to have this as a lesson for the Prince of Wales, for someone so young Edward Prince of Wales showed a remarkably sharp mind for all things philosophical. I also thought if William Caxton needed another book to print, this would be ideal for there were many who would appreciate the depth of wisdom contained in it. I wasn't aware at that moment Caxton was arranging to ship all his equipment to England in the hope of finding a wider audience for the books. It is often the way of the fates that two people can be doing two very different things and they come together as if they were meant to be.

I found solace for the grieving mind I carried in the translation work, I found more solace in some of the sayings I was working on. The experience was healing and rewarding when I handed the finished book to Caxton, to later be told it was one of the finest translations he had seen. The book was printed, people bought it, despite word going round that it was dull, but then I did not expect the average aristocrat to want to spend time studying it. It was enough for me they had a copy. I presented a copy to Edward, who showed interest in the subject for about three heartbeats and then went back to admiring the cover and the printed pages. It didn't matter. I had impressed him and that was a hard thing to do.

Ludlow was home for the Prince of Wales, his brother the duke of York, and for me. It was far enough from London for me to have an excuse not to attend every banquet and ball Edward staged, but far enough that when I did return, I saw the increasing girth of my king and worried for his constitution. It seemed he had allowed himself to grow soft, to spend too much time with Hastings, but that was a personal vendetta I never told anyone. Gloucester had grown darker and more intense, that being the only word I can find after some lengthy deliberation. I feared his devious mind and obvious love of power. He was Lord of the North and it showed.

There were dark clouds, many of them, hovering on the horizon of my life. I watched Edward grow larger and more indolent, the Soldier King long buried under the weight of excess fat, I watched Gloucester get darker by the week and wondered what was going on in that exceptional mind, how far ahead were his plans; how knowledgeable were his spies and casual informants? They were far ahead of mine, no matter how I tried to match the ones he had recruited. He had the best of them and I had the residue. But I knew enough to make plans. I began to arrange for stashes of weapons in strategic places, paying a ransom for their location to be kept secret. Even that wasn't enough, as I found later, to my cost. My sister was becoming fractious, a difficult wife to a king who was fast losing interest in everything. No battles to fight, no schemes to get involved in, he ate and drank to excess. Elizabeth had given him ten legitimate (so we thought) children, he had at least that number if not more of illegitimate children. That was the one thing which could arouse interest in him. My sister knew it and knew of those who were special to him. She didn't resent them, she was angry and infuriated by the casual bedding of young ones, knowing she could no longer compete.

If you were wondering how I knew all this, it was conveyed through a nonstop stream of letters from London to Ludlow. Under the chatter and gossip was the real reason for the letter writing, plans for the time Edward would shake off his mortal coil. She helped plan the locations for the weapons, advised on how many men at arms I would need and could get together, when her son was ready to be taken to London for his coronation. Elizabeth had inherited Mother's sharp instinctive mind and used it well.

Chapter 13 - It all falls apart

The news of Edward IV's death from tertian fever arrived by lathered horse and exhausted messenger, atop a hastily written missive from my sister instructing me to set out for London immediately with 6,000 armed men. The other messenger had no doubt reached Middleham or York, wherever Gloucester was holding court at the time. with the same information: Edward IV is dead, long live Edward V, subtitle, if he can be got there and crowned before you get there, Lord Protector. This catch-all role meant Gloucester could do all that a crowned king could do and none could dispute any of it.

I set to work finding 2,000 men. My sister's demands were too wild, would be too difficult to coordinate on the journey to London and would appear threatening.

Arrangements were hastily made, we set out early one morning, the dew still showing on everything. The boy was torn between his pride at being the king-in-waiting and sorrow for a father he only slightly knew but who was still a presence, he had been king, after all. His brother treated it as a game, riding out of the procession and having to be brought back. I set my nephew Richard Grey to watching over him. My friend Thomas Vaughan did his best to help with the retinue, some of which were inclined to linger if they saw a good-looking girl. I could see it would be a long journey and consulted with the head of the men at arms as to the best place to break for refreshments and rest.

'Stony Stratford,' he said immediately. 'Good inns, good stabling and well on our way to London, sire.' It sounded perfect – as all good plans do when they are first made. The logistics – a lovely modern expression you use so much and which says it all – render most plans obsolete immediately.

But all went well for a time, I actually began to relax and think about finishing the next book for Caxton, when we arrived at Stony Stratford to find Gloucester there with a huge retinue of armed men.

Alarm bells began ringing so loudly I could scarcely hear myself greet him and the slug (forgive me) Buckingham grinning widely and falsely alongside him. Somehow Edward and his brother were split away from our company, despite Edward demanding he stay with his Uncle Rivers, somehow I was coerced – by politeness and good manners – into agreeing to sup with the Lord Protector and the Slug that eve. Before then I had the task of arranging board and lodging for all the men and horses. It was fortunate I had stockpiled gold coins and thought to bring them with me, gold spoke louder than any words and the men were soon housed, preparing to be fed and the horses groomed and attended to. Several of them had gone lame on the ride and needed attention; a few others had cast shoes. The arrangements seemed to go on and on. It's the biggest part of the fuss and bother at the time and no one, as far as I have seen, acknowledged any of it. This brings me back to the need to remember we were and are human beings, not ciphers for you to move around a battlefield or a country, come to that. We were not picked up in Ludlow and deposited in Stony Stratford like a bunch of toy soldiers, there were hours of riding, of discomfort, of need for breaks, to check on the welfare of both men and animals... I assume that, unlike me, most historians were keen to get to the real essence of the time, Stony Stratford+Lord Protector+Buckingham (aka Slug)+removal of Edward V and his brother from the party. I had all that in mind but it fought for precedence over the men and animals that had taken us that far.

I was invited to a private meal with Gloucester and Slug. I wanted to refuse, wanted to get to bed after a pint or two of mead and some rough baked bread and cheese, but politeness dictated I had to go.

We ate, we laughed, we exchanged anecdotes about our late king and for a time it was as if Edward were still living. Gloucester's face did not change when he spoke of his dead brother, a remarkable feat of keeping his feelings locked away. Slug looked from one to the other of us, taking his cue from the way we responded to the talk, rather than initiate anything himself. I wondered why he was there.

When I went to my bed, the inn was quiet and there was no one outside.

When I rose from my bed, the inn was noisy and there was a ring of armed men around the inn. I felt my heart sink, the young king was not with me, he was obviously in the hands of the Lord Protector and I was too, in a different and I knew terminal way. I was violently sick and grateful no one saw that. They would have called me coward again if they'd known how the circumstances struck such horror into my soul.

As if I had deliberately created her image, I saw Elizabeth in my room, smiling, waving; beckoning me to her. It was all I needed to gather my strength again and even put on a smile, false as it may be. 'I won't be long joining you,' I told her and even more strength flowed into my limbs.

It was at that moment the men at arms charged into the room, arrested me, told my squire to pack my belongings and follow me – and them – to Sheriff Hutton castle.

I left my servant to pack and went with the armed men to the stables where I checked my horse carefully – time wasting – before mounting and waiting for the word to leave. We had not broken our fast, no one had mentioned that, no one offered as much as a draft of spring water but I did not ask. No way would I give any indication they had discomforted me.

Gloucester came out into the courtyard and gave what passed for a smile. "Too bad it ended like this, Rivers. If you were a reasonable person we could talk about the cache of arms everywhere, we could discuss the future of your wards, we could come to some arrangement but you are a Woodville and as such cannot be negotiated with. I won't see you again. Ratcliffe will oversee your trial and subsequent execution for treason."

Slug appeared from the stable, gave me what he must have thought was a sympathetic smile (it wasn't, it was pure malice) and mounted his fine chestnut gelding with showy grace.

They went one way, heading toward London, we were led the other way, north to Sheriff Hutton and our final days.

Chapter 14 - Those sad last days

What can you talk about with family and friend when every day is bringing you one day nearer to execution? I spent a lot of time on business, writing lengthy dispatches to my business manager, to the overseer at Sandringham and other homes we had. I wrote at length to my wife and finally drafted my will. It was that act which finally brought it home to me that this really was the end. It was at that point I asked for a cleric and a hair shirt, not necessarily in that order. I asked for a Book of Hours too, even if it tore me apart to remember reading this with my beloved Elizabeth. It almost felt like treachery to read them then but I consoled myself with the fact I was not reading them with someone else, but with the spirit who haunted my suite of rooms. I refused to think of them as prison. They were but I didn't have to admit it, did I?

During the day I spent time with my nephew and my friend Thomas. We discussed the rumours coming from London: that the marriage was invalid due to Edward's inability to allow a woman to walk away from him, no matter the devious acts he had to commit to ensure she stayed, resulting in the young king being deposed by reason of illegitimacy, of the public announcements and calls on Gloucester to take the crown. I could see, without being there, the self-satisfied face he would wear as he accepted, reluctantly, of course but how soon was the coronation arranged? How soon before he was busy issuing laws here and there and everywhere?

We were not sure what or how or why my two delightful intelligent wards seemed to disappear; no one got word to me about that. Most of our correspondence was scanned by the guards, whoever knew their fate knew better than to entrust it to the written word when it was going to be read by Gloucester's minions, loyal as long as the money flowed in the right direction.

I spent fifty seven days in Sheriff Hutton castle, time enough to hear all the rumours, to visualise all that he was doing and arranging, time enough to settle all my affairs and say my goodbyes. I was grateful for that; Warwick did not allow that small mercy to my father and brother. The fate of the Princes was the one thing I could not find out, the one thing that bothered me until I reached the spirit realms and got my answers.

The night before we were due to be moved to Pontefract Castle I wrote a long poem about my feelings. I never thought for one moment it would be anything but a way of releasing my feelings as the time of execution drew ever closer. It has been a wonderful shock and surprise to see that it has been widely read, 'translated' into relatively modern English, even set to music for medieval music folk groups! Such fame is encouraging, it should be for anyone who feels moved to write something. You never know where it might take you and your name in the years to come.

I trust you will forgive me for not dwelling overlong on the following day, 25th June. It is enough right now to say we spent the night in Pontefract castle. We had clerics and confessors if we wanted them. We were not given sustenance next morning, why should we need it? We had a moment when our guards let us out of their grasp to say our individual goodbyes before one by one we walked to the block and had Ratcliffe's pet executioner sever our heads from our bodies.

I went last. I thought it only right to do that. It was with unbelievable sadness I knelt down - and with unbelievable happiness I got up, for my Elizabeth was standing in the pools of blood in white satin shoes without a stain on them. She took my hand and we walked the white light to the realms. I was not surprised to find Richard and Thomas waiting for me, wearing huge smiles, asking why they were so afraid of dying. It was then I learned that the Princes had been rescued by the Woodvilles, who else? and were safe. Later. when they returned to the realms, I was pleased to be reunited with them, for I loved them both as if they were my own natural children. I know now they have approached the publisher of this my story, which makes it even better for me.

You have the saying 'what goes around comes around' – I think that's right. Two years after our executions, Richard III was cut down on the battlefield at Bosworth and carried off, naked, face down on someone's animal commandeered for the purpose.

My only wish now is that someone be kind enough to fund the excavation of my bones, as my channel – who is also my wife as she was then and is now – is capable of sorting my bones from those of Richard and Thomas. I would so like to lie in my own grave in Grafton, where I was happy and content, more than any other time in my relatively short life. But that I know is probably asking too much... I am happy my story is told, I am happy to be able to walk and talk and help my beloved wife. I hope you, my reader, have enjoyed reading this and that you have been given a new insight into that troubled dangerous time in English history.

I trust you have a better and kinder understanding of the Woodville clan, too!

Epilogue

Antony Wydeville, KG, Lord Scales of Newcelles and the Isle of Wight, 2nd Earl Rivers, died on the 25th June 1483, aged 41, along with his nephew Richard Gray (aged 19) and friend Thomas Vaughan, after a 'mock' trial held by Sir Robert Radcliffe, on the orders of the Lord Protector, Richard of Gloucester. These are the facts. It is, I believe, fitting for me to say that by virtue of his sister's position, Antony Wydeville attained high office, great wealth and fame. By virtue of his sister's ambitions for her son, Antony Wydeville died. It is a moot point whether you say he died, was executed or, as one noted Isle of Wight historian declared, murdered. The fact is; England lost a leading intellectual, a gifted writer and academic, a fine politician and a loyal brother and guardian on that day, whatever was at the heart of the decision to have him executed.

Historians generally dismiss Antony Wydeville as of no consequence and in truth a great Wydeville bias is firmly in place. The family is known as upstarts, popinjays and many other derogatory terms. Mostly the historical bias shows in the endless errors which occur when anyone writes about him, which indicates a lack of the proper interest that in turn leads to improper research. He is confused regularly with his father, Richard Wydeville, 1st Earl Rivers, he is dismissed as a man lacking in courage (on the basis of an alleged outburst by the king at one time) and as not being committed to his role of tutor to the young Prince of Wales. There are many more instances of character assassination throughout books on the period.

His great Tournament is a prime example of this. The original medieval report was used as the basis for that chapter, a document that in itself defies and challenges those historians who dismissed the whole thing as a showpiece, with the men exchanging no more than two or three blows before the king stopped it. That was taken from a rather cynical report by Fabyan, whereas the medieval report itself and the additional reporting by Olivier de la Marche tell a very different story. The fact at least one historian chose to only use Fabyan's version reveals a lack of research on their part, for it is obvious both from the sources already stated and yet more research on battle or poll axes that the men did considerable damage to each other's amour and created a few serious bruises too before the fight was halted. No great showpiece tournament like that would be stopped after such a short time, simply because all the spectators, the king especially, had gathered to see an exhibition of arms, not a fake fight. And, for the historians who say the tournament was a draw, again I would refer them to the original report in which it clearly states that Antony was awarded the honour of both days. To say anything else shows a clear anti-Wydeville bias. This was no mere tawdry sideshow; this was a full scale, incredibly expensive, ritualistic and meaningful emprise, ending with a clash of arms of two well-matched knights which, it is reported, was talked about by Londoners for many years. If anyone says anything different to that, remember the 'anti-Wydeville bias' that runs through so many books - and ignore it.

This confusion of historical facts is not a modern phenomenon. The Excerpta Historica, dated 1833, has the following comment in the section describing the tournament fought between Antony, Lord Scales and Antoine, Bastard of Burgundy:

'This statement shows the errors of all our historians, in asserting that the combat occurred in honour of the marriage of the King's sister Margaret, of which the first notice in the Foedera is a commission to the Earl of Warwick to treat on the subject with the

Count Charles, dated on the 22nd of March 1455, whereas the challenge had been accepted by the Bastard almost a year before, and his brother's wife died on Sept. 26, 1465. Nor was this marriage concluded until several months after the tournament. It has been misrepresented by the chroniclers, that the Bastard had been sent over to negotiate this marriage, and that he fought during his stay here; and Walpole says that Lord Scales was sent to Burgundy for the same purpose: but neither of these assertions declares that Lord Scales and he never saw each other before they met in Fleet Street. Even the year in which the tournament was fought has been differently stated.'

From this it can be seen that over the intervening years, many errors have crept into many books and have been repeated by many historians. None of them, it would seem, bother to go back to the primary sources and it is clear none go back to the person who lived at the time to get the facts direct from them. By the way, his name is spelled without the 'h'; that did not arrive in the name Antony until the end of the 16th century. There is no author (so far) who has spelled his name correctly.

The work of channelling this book was rewarding and, as Antony, Earl Rivers, became clear to me as a person, I began to appreciate his many talents and skills, his natural gifts on an intellectual level and then to realise the tragedy of his life being abruptly brought to such a sad end. I will leave the reader to decide whether the line from his ballad is correct: 'Willing to die.' All I will say is that on the 25th June 1483, Pontefract Castle became the site of the ending of an outstanding life with the death of an outstanding man.

You may well decide not to believe that this is a channelled book direct from spirit, instead to think I am a good author who wrote an interesting work of fiction, in which case I hope you enjoyed your read. If you choose to believe I channelled the work, then you will have had an insight into a period of history usually only seen through the distorted eyes of historians. There are more such insights to come from a great variety of people who have approached me with the same request, to tell their story and put the truth in front of the world.

Thank you for buying this book and for reading it to the end. If nothing else, you should have a different opinion on the man known as Antony Wydeville, which is what we set out to achieve.

Dorothy Davies,
Isle of Wight

AFTERWORD

My thanks go to:

Antony Wydeville, Earl Rivers, for entrusting me with his story, his love and his constant presence and for taking me as his wife again (I thought once would have been enough for any man);

Mary Holliday, trusted friend and adviser;

Ann-Jacqueline Davies for the stunning water colour portrait of Antony,

Corrine Cyster for the stunning pastel portrait of Antony,

Terry Wakelin, my rock and my anchor no matter which side of life he is on;

My Inner Circle for love, laughter and support throughout my days and nights.

Stuart Holland, friend and publisher, for accepting the book for publication.

And to the many, many people and organisations who offered information, found prints, advised on the legality of titles and all the complicated questions that arose as I worked with Antony to make sure that the book was absolutely right in today's world. It was right from his perspective but he is as aware as I am that modern historians, should they care to read it, also need to be able to see that the facts presented are correct. This we have done with great care because of the multitude of mistakes, oversights and sheer nonsense written about Antony, 2nd Earl Rivers and the Wydevilles generally. It would be hard to find another family more maligned without good cause. They just happened to be in the wrong place at the wrong time, it would seem. Even fiction writers manage to either get it wrong or allow their bias to show.

I freely admit to being biased, but someone needs to restore the balance...

IN MEMORIAM

A very special mention needs to be made here of those in this modern age who suffered as Antony did, a period of imprisonment with the certain knowledge at the end that their heads would be cut off.

Antony knows well the mental torment the person goes through. He also knows that there is a fear that some people will be forgotten; as time goes on our memories are blurred and people who were murdered in this way – he uses the word advisedly – will no longer be remembered by anyone outside of their family and friends. He and I wish to immortalise them.

Remembering now and always:

MARGARET HASSAN
(April 18, 1945–November 8, 2004) an Irish aid worker who had worked in Iraq for many years until she was abducted and murdered by unidentified kidnappers in Iraq in 2004, at the age of 59.

KENNETH BIGLEY
(22 April 1942 - 7 October 2004), a civil engineer who was kidnapped in Iraq on 16 September 2004, and beheaded after 'deadlines' were not met.

EUGENE ARMSTRONG
(June 5, 1953 - September 20, 2004) a civilian contractor kidnapped along with his two colleagues from a house in Baghdad on September 16, 2004. Following the expiration of a 24 hour deadline by the group's captors to have all women released from Abu Ghraib, then being held by coalition forces, he was beheaded on 20

September 2004, revealed in a video that became widely circulated across the internet following its release.

JACK HENSLEY
(September 22, 1955 – September 21, 2004) an American engineer from Georgia. While working in Iraq he was kidnapped and beheaded by terrorists. His colleague, Eugene Armstrong, was beheaded the previous day. Hours after Jack Hensley was beheaded, Tawhid and Jihad posted a videotape on the Internet of British hostage Kenneth Bigley pleading to then British Prime Minister Tony Blair to have his life spared.

NICK BERG
(April 2, 1978 – May 7, 2004) an American businessman who went to Iraq after the US invasion of Iraq. He was abducted and later beheaded according to a video released in May 2004 by Islamic militants.

KIM SUN-IL
(September 13, 1970 – c. June 22, 2004) a South Korean translator and Christian missionary who was kidnapped and beheaded in Iraq.

SHOSEI KODA
November 29, 1979 – November 3, 2004) a Japanese citizen who was kidnapped whilst touring the country and later beheaded in Iraq.

SEIF ADNAN KANAAN
(Died October 22, 2004), an Iraqi citizen who was abducted in Iraq and beheaded. The reason given by the kidnappers, the Army of Ansar Al-Sunna, was that he was employed by the United States Army.

DANIEL PEARL
(October 10, 1963 – February 1, 2002) an American journalist who was kidnapped and killed by terrorists. His murder was videotaped.

PIOTR STANACZAK
(1966 - 7 February 2009 in Attock) a Polish geologist who was beheaded by Islamic terrorists in Pakistan in February 2009.

PAUL MASHALL JOHNSTON, JNR
(May 8, 1955 – June 18, 2004) an American helicopter engineer who lived in Saudi Arabia. In 2004, he was taken hostage by terrorists and his murder recorded on video tape.

Those we have named and all the others we are not aware of,
those who were executed during and after the time this book was being written,
are in our thoughts and prayers for eternity.